The Old Man

Gloria Elias-Fallone

Cedar Publishing

The Old Man

I dedicate this story to all the migrants who left behind their precious homeland to give their children a better future. They sacrificed everything and I want to acknowledge that. To my beloved mother and father, thank you.

1

All Alone

One early winter's morning well before sunrise, a quiet street in the inner west of Sydney lays still in darkness as the neighbourhood sleeps. An old corner store stands out amongst the clutter of dwellings, a mixed business from the past, once relied on for necessities such as milk and bread. It was swallowed up years ago by large supermarkets that moved in to satisfy the demands of a new affluent mob that wedged out the old neighbourhood over time. It was once a community of migrants, middle eastern in the main, brave young adults that left their cherished homeland to start a new life. Over time they got old, many sold up and moved in with their children, they would care for their parents until the end. The yuppies waited like vultures, ready to swoop down the moment a sale sign appeared, snapping up another piece of prime real estate.

Yet the old derelict corner store is still standing, albeit disconcertingly amongst large, embellished homes, exquisitely renovated with pruned gardens and thick green lawns trimmed perfectly. To the displeasure of the neighbours, this old store looks neglected and out of place, boarded shut with cheap wooden panelling that covers up old signage painted across the shop front; the sign barely visible now as it has weathered over time. But the store stands out for other reasons, perched amongst a slumbering string of homes, someone stirs quietly within the old shop. The room sits deathly still in darkness, save for the faint glow of a lamp fixed to the wall that illuminates a ghostly silhouette of Elias hunched over in his chair. Elias is a very old man who appears light years away in thought, maybe reliving memories of the past. Rather than slumber in the comfort of his own bed, he sits alone in the dark corner of a derelict store.

Elias called it quits years ago when he decided to close the store down for good. Everything in the shop is run down, from the faded bushell's tea sign painted on the wall, to the dusty shelving, purpose built by Elias back in the day when he was stronger and able. Even an old fridge covered in Coca Cola stickers stands gathering dust, completely empty but still standing with no purpose. An old freezer sits idle and bare, back in the day when business boomed it was filled to the brim with ice-creams, enjoyed by customers over the hot summer months. Nothing made Elias happier than a profitable business, where lots of money could be made.

Back in the day, he was an ambitious man, a young immigrant with big dreams and an unwavering drive to start a new life in Australia, the 'lucky country.' Hungry for an abundance of wealth and prosperity, he worked very hard, leaving little time for his wife and the children that came soon after their marriage, such was the way back then, especially in the Lebanese culture. In his view he provided well, despite never being around much at all. That was his stand, what he believed, but it was not how his family saw things, and in the end, it did not serve him well to think the way he did. And now he sits alone in failing health, with no one around to care for him.

As he sits and remembers the past, colour drains from his face, leaving him looking ghostly white. Suddenly Elias slumps over and slides out of his chair ending up on the floor. He lays lifeless and weak with no strength left to lift himself up or call out for help, but he doesn't panic. Instead, he stares into space as his eyes slowly close shut and all at once he lays deathly still in darkness.

Elias lays lifeless in a hospital bed and slips in and out of consciousness, each shallow breath he takes brings him closer to the end. With little time left, he thinks about his life, the memories are haunting him. He suffered terribly throughout life, much of the anguish brought on by his own choices, but not all. The way it came to this can only be understood by knowing how his life began, many years ago.

In 1901 a baby girl named Leila is born into a poor family of farmers, they reside in a village community in Greater Syria, later to be known as Lebanon following the breakdown of the territory. As she takes her first breath Leila belts out a loud cry that startles both mother and midwife. A strong pair of lungs like hers would normally be cause for celebrations, a sign of good health. Even so, her mother's heart sinks into a state of deep despair. She will have to deliver bad news to her husband, they will weep together over another failed attempt to produce a baby boy, a son to carry on the family name, an heir to one day takeover their modest family farm.

And so, the prospect of not having anyone to run the family farm becomes more and more a reality, a future of extreme poverty is certain to follow in the years to come without a son. Accordingly, there is no reason to celebrate the birth of a beautiful healthy baby girl, sadly, they consider it a time to mourn. Their custom rules that a woman's role is to bear and raise children and take care of the family home, not run a farm. Leila's parents now have seven daughters and no son, their desperate prayers go unanswered, but they will keep trying, they must.

2
The Old Country

At fifteen years of age Leila has grown into a beautiful young woman, gifted with striking Mediterranean blue eyes, flawless olive brown skin, and silky soft golden-brown hair draped long down her back. Leila's betrothal will be an easy feat for her parents, there is no doubt about it. They have married off all their other daughters to acceptably suitably men from the village, but none into a family of wealth. All the eligible men from the village are spellbound by Leila's beauty, and her parents plan to take full advantage of this valuable opportunity to escape poverty, she will marry into money, they've made no bones about it. To her parent's dismay and disapproval, Leila only has eyes for her best friend since childhood, Joseph is the man she loves.

Two years older than Leila, Joseph is no less striking than his beloved and stands out easily as the most handsome man in the village. Unusually tall for a middle eastern man, he is strong and lean in stature, graced with eyes as deep blue as Leila's, a common feature of the northern Lebanese native. Leila and Joseph are young and naive, giddy over their unlikely intimate union as husband and wife, longing for the family they'll have together. Leila begs her parents to choose Joseph as her betrothed, but they outright refuse. Joseph comes from a poor family and her parents won't allow him stand in the way of their only chance to escape a life of poverty, an opportunity to put an end to a cruel cycle that has plagued their family for generations.

In resolute defiance, Leila refuses to marry at all, she protests that if she can't be with Joseph then she will be with no one at all. Sadly, her naivety fails her, preventing her from anticipating the cruel beatings that ensue at the hands her father, a price she pays for her disobedience. Joseph knows nothing of the beatings, Leila would never dare to tell. She knows he would seek to protect her and that would cause more problems. Leila has given much thought to running away and eloping with Joseph, but in the end, she would be disowned by her family for it. Worse still, her actions would bring the entire family's reputation into disrepute, their meagre social standing within the village would dwindle away even further. After weeks of brutal beatings, she has no more strength left to fight, and more than that, Leila is unwilling to risk her families good name by eloping, devastated, she reluctantly accepts her marriage to Joseph is not to be. She must succumb to her parents' wishes, she will marry whoever they choose, even at the cost of losing her true love.

Just as she prepares to concede defeat, Leila overhears her parents talk quietly in the kitchen about a famine that has spread across their country. They whisper nervously about the great famine of Mount Lebanon crippling their economy, even the wealthiest of families have lost their fortunes and suddenly all prospects of escaping poverty through their daughter vanish. To Leila's delight and utter relief, her parents decide she should marry Joseph, at least in this case they know their daughter will be happy.

Accordingly, at the age of fifteen, Leila marries Joseph and just under a year later their first and only child is born. The proud parents are blessed with the birth of a healthy baby boy, whom they name Elias. They shower him with boundless love and affection, smiling proudly and joyfully at his every move. Apart from work, Joseph takes his son everywhere, he can't bare being apart from him and this fills Leila's heart with utter joy.

Before long Leila and Joseph are eager to expand their family, sadly the famine has worsened leaving the village to face a crippling poverty. Very few families can afford even the necessities like bread and milk, heartbreakingly, their plans to have more children must wait. Joseph takes any work he can, sometimes labouring day and night and often for next to no pay, with each passing day the work dries up. All the while Joseph refuses to give up, all he can think about is putting food on the table for his son and wife. Their extended families are struggling as well, just like most of the village.

By the time Elias is two years old the great famine has completely ravaged the country, the economy is all but destroyed. The Ottoman

Government has only made things worse by pouring everything into the military effort, all food is redirected to their defence, and only the very rich can buy off the black market. Sadly, it means families like Leila and Joseph's are forced to starve.

By now happier times are all but a distant memory for Joseph and Leila, their daily lives begin to play out like a nightmare. There is no food left in the village, families are forced to fight to survive, the sight of villagers sorting through rubbish for food has become common-place. The handful of wealthy families lucky enough to buy food off the black market have their garbage bins combed through by the less fortunate, some have not eaten for days, and others not for weeks.

Months pass by and things only get worse. Joseph and Leila do all they can to save their son from the grips of starvation. Already many people in the village have died from the famine, including members of both Leila and Joseph's families. Every morsel of food the couple can get their hands on goes to Elias first and then they eat whatever is left.

By the end of the year Leila and Joseph have lost their entire extended families to starvation, it's a miracle they have survived, although just barely. Leila watches her husband grow thinner by the day, more-so than herself and she can't understand why, they eat the same, which is next to nothing. She is unaware that Joseph has been giving all his food to Elias over the past few weeks. Despite his emaciated body of skin and bones, Joseph refuses to eat. Watching his own son starve is much more painful, and so he does whatever he can to ensure Elias survives. When Leila sleeps Joseph gives his portion of food to Elias, and this bestows him some peace. The extreme hunger pangs are a small sacrifice for a father who hopes this will be what it takes to save his son's life. Severely malnourished, Joseph dies a few days later.

Devastated by her loss, Leila can't imagine how she will go on. She suffers terrible grief over the loss of her beloved husband, as well as her extended family. Elias cries constantly, not just from hunger, but also because he can't understand where his father has gone. Joseph died when Elias slept and Leila buried him along with all the other corpses, careful of her son not to see, now Elias has no idea where his father has gone. Plagued with anguish Leila can't sleep or think straight but knows she must push through her crippling grief for Elias to stand a chance of survival. Day and night she agonises over the thought of how she will provide for her son. She has no money or food and no idea how to get it. All she can do is pray, and she does this day and night.

As it happens Leila's prayers are answered, three years into the devastating famine, there is finally some light at the end of the tunnel. The village church and many others like it receive much needed help, thanks to a benevolent act of kindness from a Lebanese community in Egypt. Their life-saving charity means food supplies can be channelled through to the Lebanese mainland. If not for their efforts Leila's entire village would have perished. The village church can finally help its people, and one morning a nun comes knocking on Leila's door only to find mother and son harrowingly malnourished, it has been just under two weeks since they last ate. The nun takes Leila and Elias into the convent and sees through their lengthy recovery.

Many months pass before Leila and Elias recover physically, but the emotional toll of their experience remains for a lifetime. Forever indebted to the nun who came knocking on her door that deathly grim morning, Leila decides to devote herself completely to the church. She rarely ventures outside of the convent or church, which have become her sanctuary, the church has filled a deep dark void in her life. Although Leila still grieves terribly over the loss of her beloved husband, and extended family, her son and the church have saved her.

Sadly, things don't pan out the way Leila hopes, committing her life to the church is not to be. Being one of very few women of childbearing age left in the village, she is still considered marriage worthy, even as a widow and mother. Leila wants to remain in the convent, hoping to help the nuns and raise her son here. The nuns have other ideas, although they care deeply for Leila and Elias, there are other families in the village that have no prospect of support without the church. Leila on the other hand could remarry, and this would guarantee mother and child their livelihood.

The local priest and all the nuns have become guardians in some ways to the families living under their roof. And so, it's not surprising to see that a parishioner has already asked about Leila, they are desperate to find a suitable wife for their son Nadeem. Accordingly, the priest arranges a meeting between the parents, and the prospective bride and groom. Despite Leila's status as a widow with a child of her own, the family remain intent on pursuing the prospect. They have no other choice because there are so few women left in the village for their son to choose from, at least that's the explanation they offer. Tragically for Leila they don't reveal the truth about Nadeem, which would easily explain why he can't find a bride. Their son is an unpleasant and nasty man, he is also much older than Leila, but that doesn't seem to be an issue for anyone, save for poor Leila. Unlike her, the other eligible women in the village are lucky enough to have a surviving member of their family investigate the reasons behind Nadeem's challenge to find a bride. There is no such person to protect Leila, all her family perished during the famine and the church don't consider asking questions about Nadeem's character, arranging a betrothal is not something they have done before. They unknowingly encourage Leila to accept this arrangement because it guarantees her and Elias a livelihood and it means the church can offer her room up to someone in more need. Leila is deeply saddened by the prospect of a betrothal, reluctant to remarry so soon after her beloved husband's passing. She also worries about how Nadeem will treat her son, the most precious person in her life.

The only good thing to come out of the union would be the wealth Nadeem's family have managed to hold onto. They come from a long line of prosperous shop owners and some of that wealth has remained despite the famine, although much of it has been lost. His father has tried multiple times to arrange his son's betrothal and their wealth is never enough to broker the marriage. Not only is Nadeem a nasty person, but he is also far from handsome. He is short and fat, with dark beady eyes. He is the opposite to Joseph in all possible ways.

As it happens, Nadeem doesn't want to marry Leila, he thinks marrying a non-virgin who already has a child is well beneath him.

But in the end his hand is forced, held hostage by his parent's threat to cut off him off financially should he not go ahead with the marriage. They are yearning for grandchildren, and desperate to get Nadeem off their hands. And so, he has little choice but to follow through with the marriage, Nadeem won't surrender wealth and his social standing, his ego is far too big. Sadly, Leila and Elias become the target of Nadeem's resentment, he blames them for being forced into the marriage, even though he agrees to marry to preserve his entitlements. The deal is done, Leila will marry Nadeem, an arrangement that will create much sadness for both mother and child in the years to come.

3

A Turn For The Worst

There are no surprises then that the newlyweds feel the strain of an unhappy marriage right from the start, nevertheless both have a vested interest in making the marriage work, they try to set aside their disappointments and focus on making this arrangement work. Although this is Leila's ticket out of poverty, she struggles to accept how her new husband treats Elias.

At first, she tries to turn a blind eye to the many cruel remarks Nadeem makes about her son, like calling him a baby for crying at night or mocking him for clinging to her skirt whenever Nadeem's family visit. Nadeem shows no empathy, despite knowing the child has only recently lost his father, and an entire extended family. He knows perfectly well why Elias cries at night and is shy around the step grandparents he barely knows, but Nadeem doesn't care. All that matters is how this has affected him, and he resents Leila and her child for the predicament they have placed him in. Even worse, he never misses an opportunity to remind Leila that Elias is not his child, that he is some other man's son.

One night following a terrifying nightmare, Elias runs to his mother's bedside crying inconsolably, begging her to come sleep with him in his bed. Leila hugs her son tightly in a desperate effort to console him, hoping and praying Nadeem doesn't awaken, but it's too late.

'What is wrong with this boy?' He screams at both of them.

Startled, Leila holds her son tighter as he trembles in her arms, terrified by Nadeem's abruptness.

'Go back to your bed.' He yells at the terrified child. 'You're not a baby, but you act like one.'

Leila has heard enough; she springs to her feet holding Elias tightly as he cries in her arms. She heads off out of their room but suddenly turns back to face Nadeem, and in a rare act of defiance she defends her son.

'He has nightmares because he misses his father.' She snaps at him, but instantly regrets it.

Nadeem stares venomously at mother and child but couldn't be bothered to get out of bed. Instead, he mumbles hurtful comments, hoping that hurts.

'I don't care, that's your problem. He is not my son.'

Leila can't fathom how a man could be this cruel, but she has no hope of changing him, all she can do is try and protect her son. She covers his ears hoping to block out the abusive verbal attack.

'You treat him like a baby, I would never raise my son like that.' Nadeem lashes out, infuriating Leila but she can't fight back out of fear.

'He is not even three years old yet, try to understand.' She leaves the room with Elias in her arms fuming with rage, but she doesn't retaliate afraid to cause any further trouble.

'What a hopeless mother you are.' He scolds Leila, but she refuses to bite back, stakes are too high. Leila takes Elias to his room and Nadeem goes back to sleep.

She lays in bed next her son and holds him closely hoping to calm him so he can fall back to sleep. Elias holds his mother tightly.

'When will father come back?' He asks, still too young to understand the concept of death. Leila's heart sinks in despair, she doesn't have the strength to explain, not tonight.

'One day son, but not for a very long time, you will see you father again I promise.' She kisses him affectionately on the forehead. Elias begins to dose off but still has questions.

'Does he hate me?' He asks heavy-eyed glancing in the direction of where Nadeem sleeps.

'No, don't be silly. He is cranky because he wants to sleep, that's all. Try and understand for your mother my darling son.' She lies, hoping to protect him from the truth.

Leila knows how traumatic the past two years have been for her son, she has done everything possible to protect him. Now more than ever she regrets marrying Nadeem because he is making matters worse. But she has no control over this awful predicament, if she stands up to Nadeem, she risks their livelihood. She is terrified of facing a life of destitution, they had already come terrifyingly close to that. Yet if Nadeem continues to abuse her son like this it will have a grave effect on him, she grapples with this heart-wrenching reality. For now, Leila tries not to think about it, she must do her best to appease Nadeem in the hope that he'll change. For now, all she can do his shower Elias with her boundless love, an easy feat for a mother that adores her child. She will try to make up for what Elias has lost, a father that cherished his son so much he starved for him; and for the grandparents that adored him, and the aunts and uncles that doted over their nephew. Even still, she prays day and night that one day Nadeem will learn to love Elias as his own, although she doubts that will ever be.

In line with their pledge, Nadeem's parents gift him with the two general stores for going ahead with the marriage. Accordingly, Leila and Elias now enjoy all the comforts their village community could only dream about. Nice clothes, quality foods and a large home perched high up in the hills. Notwithstanding, it comes at a heavy cost, life with Nadeem has not improved, rather it has gotten worse. Regardless, Leila endures the hardship, too afraid of being thrown back into a life of destitution. Although the famine has ended, she knows that without any family of her own, she and her son would have nowhere to go if Nadeem left. Perhaps the convent would take them in again, but that would depend on whether they had room or not, the thought of it haunts her daily. And so, this fear sows deep within and it drives Leila to do whatever she must to make Nadeem happy, to never give him any reason to leave her and Elias. It is no surprise then that Leila is delighted to discover she is pregnant just over a year after their marriage. She prays for a son knowing this will please her husband no end, it would mean he could leave his mark, the legacy of his name.

When Leila gives birth to their first child, a baby boy Nadeem can't contain his excitement, he is completely overjoyed and filled with pride. He hasn't just become a father for the first time, he is now father to a son, importantly a son of his own flesh. He insists on calling their son Charbel, named after his own father and grandfather. Nadeem's parents hold a large celebration, inviting all the village community along to honour the birth of their grandson. Elias has just turned four and is old enough to notice the fuss his stepfather makes over Charbel, the attention he gives to the new baby is in sharp contrast to how he has been treated. Elias can't recall a time when his stepfather showed him any affection, but now Nadeem won't leave his new baby son's side, showering him with endless hugs and kisses. This upsets Elias and he complains to his mother about it.

'Why does he hate me?' Elias asks his mother.

'Don't be silly, your father loves you?' She brushes off the painful truth.

'Nadeem loves the baby, he hugs and kisses him, but never me. Why mother?' He asks in frustration.

'Please stop calling him Nadeem, call him your father.' She insists, frustrated and uncomfortable with the discussion.

'But he said not to call him father?' Elias is genuinely confused.

'Only when he is angry, not always.' She tries to convince her poor son that he is loved.

If he loves me, why won't he hug and kiss me like he does with the baby?' He stares distraughtly at his mother. Leila tries hard to hide her fury, she wants to scream at Nadeem and scold him for his mistreatment of Elias, but she can't. Instead, she is forced to lie to protect him from feeling unloved.

'Charbel is a baby, the baby is tiny and cute, that's why your father gives him all the attention.' She tries hard to convince him.

'Did my other father love me?'

Leila struggles to respond, it's painful to talk about the man she loved deeply. Elias now knows his father is dead, she had to tell him in the end, he was asking too many questions. For the first time Leila begins to speak openly about the man she adored, no matter how painful, Leila must tell Elias what he deserves to know, that his father loved him with all his heart. She stares lovingly at her son, trying hard to hold back her tears.

'Of course he loved you, he barely left your side son.' Heartbroken, she remembers her true love like it was yesterday.

'Not only did your father adore you, but so did your grandmother and grandfather and all your aunties and uncles. They loved you so much, just like I do, you are so special my dear son.

Elias stares sadly at his mother because he knows these are painful memories.

'It's ok mother, I have you and that is enough.' He smiles lovingly at her.

She wipes her tears away smiling lovingly at her son, such a selflessness boy she muses, in stark contrast to his awful stepfather.

Elias wants to make his mother happy, so he decides to try his hardest to love his new brother, and starts by kissing Charbel on the forehead, Leila smiles proudly at him. She hides her anguish that eats away at her, knowing Elias will never experience the same unconditional and deep love Joseph had for him, certainly not from Nadeem.

Over the years Leila does everything she can to make sure Elias feels included and loved in their family, but Nadeem doesn't hide his strong love and affection for Charbel, his son by blood. Nadeem's unashamed nepotism becomes so obvious that Elias can easily see through his mother's cover ups, soon there will be nothing she can say to hide the truth.

No matter how hard Elias tries to impress his stepfather, the effort goes unnoticed, inevitably breaking his spirit and destroying any self-confidence he has left. Deeply hurt, this eats away at him, and from a very early age Elias begins to resent his little brother, upstaging him at every opportunity. As it happens, this merely fuels Nadeem's dislike for his stepson and leads to further mistreatment. The scars never heal and the abuse haunts Elias right throughout his life, affecting him as a person, a husband, and a father in the most damaging way.

Over a decade passes and their family has grown larger with three daughters, Nayla, Zahra, and Samya added to their brood. In 1936 the family enjoy a comfortable life in the small mountainous village of

Mount Lebanon. They reside amidst a landscape of ancient cobble stone homes spread across mountainous terrain of rolling green hills. Their large backyard boasts a striking countryside of vast timeworn land.

Elias and Charbel are now 17 and 14 years of age respectively, blessed with their mother's gene pool. They have inherited the same deep blue eyes, tan olive skin and golden-brown hair. Both fit and strong young men, Charbel bares no resemblance to his father. With their mother's good looks and their father's wealth, they will have the luxury of choice when time comes to choose a bride among the many pretty girls in their village. This pleases Nadeem no end, knowing his family is envied by all the families in their village. Sadly, that's the extent of praise Nadeem affords Elias, meanwhile he continues to find fault in almost everything else his stepson does.

The boys work hard for their father in the general store, often carting produce from farmland to the store. On this blistering hot summer afternoon Elias and Charbel struggle up the hillside weighed down by the large sack of potatoes each of them carries across their shoulders. The mesh bag digs deep into the skin weighed down by 20 kilos of spuds. They have made numerous trips today gathering stock for the general store. Sweating under the sweltering heat for hours as they undertake heavy labour, the brothers finally reach the general store and eagerly enter the cool sanctuary built from cobblestone to shelter from the hot sun. Unfortunately, they have returned later than expected and must meet their fate. Nadeem waits angrily at the entrance of the store seething as he gets ready to pounce.

'Why did you take so long?' He shouts at Elias. 'You fool, I told you I needed the potatoes this morning. We missed the trade of the day because of you.'

'It wasn't just me who travelled to and from the fields. Elias defends himself.

'Stop blaming your brother and take some responsibility, you are older than him.' He barks back.

Disheartened and aggrieved by the constant criticism, Elias doesn't hold back no matter how threatening Nadeem seems.

'You find fault in everything I do, if I were younger, it would be my fault. I'm not good enough for you, why not just say that.'

'How dare you speak to me like that? I am the head of this family.' Nadeem shouts.

Elias has had enough; he is sick and tired of the unfair treatment but doesn't speak back knowing he'll have to endure more of the badgering. Charbel looks away, extremely uncomfortable with the unfair abuse targeted at his brother, but he is too afraid to defend Elias. He is terrified of his father so stays quiet staring at the floor.

'Are you going to cry like a girl or prove to me you can be responsible like an older brother should'. Nadeem continues his attack.

'Don't compare me to a girl, old man.' Elias snaps at him.

With that Nadeem flies off the handle and back hands Elias across the mouth. On impact bright red blood spurts out from his lip. Elias stares furiously at Nadeem, loathing him, but he does not retaliate. He knows how crazy his stepfather can get so he makes his way out of the store. as Elias heads out Nadeem continues his assault.

'Go cry to your mother like a baby.' He spits out venomously, but Elias has already left the store.

'You stay and help me; we need to stock the store in preparation for tomorrow's trade.' He demands.

Chabel nods obediently, all the while keeping his head down as he trembles in fear. Although extremely distraught for his brother, he won't say a word, he's terrified.

Elias hurries into a cobblestone cottage to escape the midday heat and feels instant relief from the hot sun. He is too distracted with fury to admire this impressive structure they call home, a magnificent dwelling, centuries old, and no doubt handed down from one generation to another. The solid sandstone structure provides the family respite from the relentless summer heat, a welcome luxury for Leila and her girls who spend most of their day at home. Elias finds his mother by the stove preparing the evening meal, she smiles warmly at her son until she notices the laceration on his lip.

'What happened?' She asks deeply concerned.

'Nothing mother, I just knocked my lip trying to lift a sack of potatoes over my shoulder, that's all.' He lies to protect her.

'Another fight with your father?' Leila says enraged by the never-ending heartache Nadeem causes.

'We didn't get the potatoes to the store on time, but of course all the fault lies with me, not Charbel, even though we left together and came back to the store together, I can't do anything to please that man.'

'So, he hit you for that? I can't accept it; I will talk to him.' She says nervously.

'No, I can't put you at risk, he's a monster. I called him an old man, that's why he hit me. I would do it again, it felt good to see him hurt.'

Leila sobs helplessly, distraught by Nadeem's cruelty, she has made endless attempts to protect Elias, but it has never been enough to shield her son, to protect him from the damaging effects of abuse. Since marrying Nadeem, she has tried to appease him, hoping that might soften his heart and lead him to form an affection for Elias, to hopefully love him like a son. It never happened, nothing changed, and Leila is heartbroken. Elias hugs his mother, upset by the pain she has endured for so many years.

'You have to avoid him as much as you can, it's the only way son.' She begs him as she sobs.

'Please stop mother, I'm not a child anymore, stop trying to protect me. You are so kind and loving but I hate seeing you burdened with the responsibility of protecting me, all my life you have done that. I'm a man now mother, let me defend myself, I am capable of it.' He demands.

Leila is heartbroken, she knows Elias is right but how can a mother just give up on their beloved child? It's impossible for her, she will always try and protect him from Nadeem, at least as much as she can. She worries constantly about what he might do if she defends Elias, terrified he will retaliate by forcing Elias out of the family home. He is old enough now, so she knows Nadeem could do it if he wanted to. Elias can read the worry in his mother's face so decides to change the subject.

'Tell me about my real father, I don't remember anything about him.' He remarks.

'Please don't ask me now.' Leila looks frightened.

'He is at the shop, no one can hear.' He reassures her.

'You sisters might listen, please son.' She begs him nervously.

Elias sees the fear in her eyes but wants to know about his father.

'We'll talk quietly.' He whispers.

Leila hesitates but nods reluctantly, knowing he will not yield.

'Did he like spending time with me?' He asks solemnly.

'How many times have I told you? Why don't you believe me? Your father adored you, why would you think differently?' She shakes her head in disbelief.

Elias looks sad, how can he believe it? After years of being the target of Nadeem's brutality he struggles to accept that anyone could care about him, maybe he is as bad as his stepfather insists. Besides this, his mother has always bent the truth about Nadeem, assuring her son that he did care about him when that was not the case at all. Perhaps his mother was not telling the truth about his real father, he is filled with doubt, and it eats away at him. Leila struggles to convince her son that his birth fathers loved him undeniably; there seemed to be no way of freeing him from the damage his beastly stepfather inflicted on him over many years. Left with no choice Leila must tell him something she has always kept from Elias.

'We had very little food during the famine, sometimes there was nothing for days. Your father wouldn't eat anything, even when I begged him, I didn't want him to starve. Whatever he had, it was spared for you.' Wiping tears from her face she stares intently at her son.

'I don't say this to hurt you, but he died so you could live. Of course, he loved you.' She is distraught, forced to relive painful memories that she has tried to bury over the years, but she can remember it all, like it was yesterday. Elias is saddened knowing how difficult this is for his mother to talk about, but he has put up with feeling unloved by

Nadeem for so long, it warms his heart knowing how much his real father loved him.

'Thank you, I know how hard it is for you to talk about this, but finally I do believe that my father loved me.' He smiles lovingly at her.

Elias stares nervously at Leila, there is more he needs to get off his chest. She reads him like a book and sighs.

'What?' She asks.

'I can't keep living here.' He finally offloads the secret that has weighed heavily on his mind for months. Leila can't believe what she is hearing, annoyed and angered by her son's crazy thinking.

'What's wrong with you? Why would you even think about leaving your home? I know he is a monster, but you stand to lose everything if you go.' She whispers loudly, still nervous her daughters might hear.

'Look at your home, it's beautiful, anyone from the village would love to live here. And you have a good job, where would you find work anywhere else?' You have a choice to marry any girl from our village when you are ready. If you leave now, you will lose all that son, think about what you are doing.' She insists, trying hard to keep her voice down.

'It's not my home and I hate working for him. How will I ever become successful if I stay in my brother's shadow? I want to get a job in Beirut.' He insists.

'Where would you live? You don't know anybody there.' She whispers loudly in frustration.

'I know where I can get a job and I will find a place to live.' He insists.

'Please don't leave.' She begs him tearfully. 'I lost your father, my parents, all my sisters. Don't leave me son, please.' She begs as she sobs.

Elias looks distraught seeing his mother hurt like this.

'Ok, ok, please stop crying.' He begs her as he sighs unhappily. 'I will stay for as long as my patience will allow it, but I can't stay here much longer, I need to get away from him, otherwise I will never be happy.' He insists.

'Ok, but wait until you are a bit older, please.' She begs him, feeling an instant sense of relief.

Elias nods reluctantly and his mother smiles hugging her boy tightly. He is frustrated and disappointed but can't stand to see his mother suffer like this.

Their village is as ancient as the cedar trees that line the mountainous landscape. Cobblestone homes, hundreds of years old stand amongst the vast lush green hills. Narrow roads and pathways spiral through the terrain as a route for donkeys to move goods and villagers around, meanwhile most of the community travel by foot. The esteemed village church sits high up in the hillside, its magnificent sandstone structure centuries old is well preserved by generous donations from the community.

The village inhabitants are deeply religious people of the Maronite Catholic faith. They congregate at church each morning to worship God. This morning, like every other Leila rushes to get her daughters ready for church, and then school straight after mass. Nayla, Zahra, and Samya are growing up, now aged 11, 10 and 9 in that order. Nayla is the mirror image of her mother, unfortunately her sisters resemble their father, and are not blessed with the same good looks as their sister.

Leila must dress her girls in their finest clothing for church to show a sign of respect, a big challenge for a daily routine. If she doesn't follow customary obligations such as this, she will risk falling prey to judgement. She knows this is ridiculous, certain that Jesus would denounce their sanctimonious behaviour, even so she knows better not to say a word.

Nadeem, Elias and Charbel will meet Leila and the girls at church once the early morning trade ends. Many from the village rush to the store at dawn to gather fresh bread and other essential staples before church so they have enough food for their daily meals. This morning Leila panics because she can't find Nayla, but she has a good idea where she might find her. Nayla has an unusual obsession with the church, she is extraordinarily devout, and Leila is certain that's where she will find her oldest daughter. No other girls in the village acts like this which worries Leila because she knows Nayla will be harshly judged for it, the community always looks down on non-conformist. This hypocrisy angers Leila, her daughter's devotion to the church should be admired, not looked down upon. Instead, Nayla is laughed at because girls her age should be playing with their friends and showing interest in learning about all that is necessary to one day marry a good man and have children. Unlike his wife, Nadeem condemns even the slightest deviation from what is considered acceptable in their community and berates Leila if she questions the craziest of village norms. Driven by ego he vehemently upholds customs and traditions, despite how illogical or hypocritical. He wants to be admired as a respectable member of the community, held in high regard, and does whatever it takes to secure that standing.

With Zahra and Samya dressed, Leila hurries out of the house with both girls in tow, heading in the direction of the village church to hopefully locate her oldest daughter. They hurry down the street towards the town centre and five minutes later reach their destination. Out of breath, Leila and her girls enter and thankfully the church is empty, her daughter won't be judged on this occasion. Leila quickly spots Nayla who is kneeling at the front pew praying peacefully. The look of relief on her mother's face is instant and Leila hurries to the front of the church. She gives Nayla a soft clip across the ear snapping her out of deep prayer.

'What's wrong with you?' Leila hisses at her disobedient daughter. The church is empty, but Leila still whispers in this sacred place of worship. Nayla looks startled but holds her head down in shame.

'I just want to pray mother, before all the people come. It's so peaceful when the church is empty, and it brings me close to God.' She explains in the hope her mother might understand.

'Why can't you be like all the other girls your age? You pray like an old woman preparing to pass into the next life.'

'I want to be with our Heavenly Father and all the Saints. I look forward to the day I enter his heavenly kingdom. I want is to devote myself to God, I want to be a nun mother.'

'Don't talk like that you silly girl, you know it fills your father with rage.' Leila shakes her head in frustration. 'You will marry a good man when you are older and have lots of children. A nun's life will deny you of such joy.'

'I pray all the time that I may serve our Heavenly Father and I dearly hope to become a nun one day.' Nayla stares earnestly at her cranky mother.

The church begins to fill with worshippers and Leila takes Nayla by the arm and they quickly head to the back of the church and pile into a pew near the door. Luckily Nadeem has only just arrived, and Leila manages to avoid any confrontation from him as to what just happened, he strongly disapproves of Nayla's aspired vocation. He has made it clear on many occasions that he objects to Nayla's extreme devotion to the church, he wants all his children to marry and have children and, in that way, continue the family legacy.

When the mass ends all the parishioners spill out of the church and into the courtyard to gather. With the morning rush over Nadeem and the boys won't need to hurry straight back to the store, instead they join the congregation. Most of the villager's hover around one another to gloat about their successes, contradicting the humble and selfless teachings of the mass that only just ended. For many this is their opportunity to boast about acquired wealth or the birth of a baby boy. Leila worries about Elias and Charbel spending time around people like this, she fears over their terrible influence. She descends from a humble and poor family and resents the notion that anybody should regard themselves better than another.

As it happens, she has no cause for concern, because all those braggers have their days of opulence numbered. The rippling effects of the Great Depression and impending Second World War begins to gnaw away at Lebanon's economy. The family wealth Nadeem has enjoyed for generations will soon disappear and for the first time in his life he will need to go without. He has no idea that the impending hardship is already creeping closer to his doorstep.

As the country's economy crumbles the flow on effect hits Nadeem like a blow to the head. The worsening financial hardship cuts to the bone, and Nadeem becomes even more miserable to be around. As he gets worse, Elias and Leila are targeted, they sit front and centre of the firing line of his insults and aggression. The family have lost the bulk of their wealth with the once prosperous general store no longer turning over much of a profit, and the other store forced to close. This has left Nadeem a poor man, an unbearable blow to an enormous ego. Subsequently he is awful to be around, especially when he drinks, which is often now. His parents have lost all their riches, ending generations of wealth, the experience feels like a nightmare, and they dream of waking up to the life of yesteryear.

By now Elias and Charbel are young adults, while Nayla, Zahra and Samya are well into their teenager years. The girls no longer go to school and have taken on domestic chores helping their mother around the house, such is their custom. The crippling effects of a failed economy has driven many of the young men out of the village to seek work abroad. Many of the men have bravely ventured off as far as Brazil, Argentina, Canada, and the USA, with some going as far as Australia. This causes more strain on the family because now there are fewer eligible men left as marriage prospects for their ageing daughters. Nadeem's family no longer have the wealth they used to have, the one thing that could have helped in bargaining a marriage for his daughters. Nayla counts this as a blessing, an answer to her prayers, so for now she breathes a small sigh of relief, hoping this means she is a step closer to fulfilling her dream of becoming a nun.

Elias holds onto hopes and dreams that are in stark contrast to Nayla, but both have chosen paths that infuriate Nadeem. Elias wants to follow in the footsteps of those who have already left their village in pursuit of a better life overseas, where the prospects of building wealth is very real. He knows this will be the only way out of a life of poverty, but Nadeem forbids it, demanding that Elias continue working in the store. Despite the slow trade, there is still a steady flow of business, so he needs his son and stepson to work and won't hire someone from outside the family to replace him, fearing they'll dip their hand in the till. This constraint fills Elias with rage, he considers it a ploy by his stepfather to prevent him from becoming successful in his own right, which is true. He desperately wants to escape the life that has held him back for too many years, he dreams of leaving for a land with endless opportunities, affording him a chance to build a fortune of his own. Elias is certainly not afraid of the hard work, nor the long hours that awaits him should he go; and the uncertainties of the unknown fill him with excitement rather than fear. He longs to escape his stepfather's abuse, which he has tolerated since childhood. More than ready to move on, he begins to plot his escape eager to leave everything behind, apart from his mother and sisters.

To help the family make ends meet Elias takes work wherever he can get it, this is in addition to working in their general store. Charbel works exclusively for his father which strikes Leila as unfair given Elias is working multiple jobs, but of course she is too scared to say anything. It doesn't bother Elias at all because it means he sees less of Nadeem; besides he has been pocketing a portion of the wages from those extra jobs without telling anyone. By working the other jobs, he makes a lot of new friends, most of them live outside of his village. Importantly for Elias many of them are planning to migrate overseas and he listens intently on how they plan to achieve that; this is how he comes to conceive his own plot to flee his small village for a land far away.

Months pass and Elias forges strong ties with his workmates, so much so that they ask him to join them on a journey to Australia in the coming months. Dizzy with excitement at the prospect of leaving, Elias knows this means he will have to leave a lot earlier than planned. Nevertheless, he prefers to make the journey with friends rather than set off on his own. With the impending journey taking place sooner than expected he has lots of questions. He fires away with question after question at his friends, wanting to know how they plan to set themselves up once they arrive in the new world. Saib, the natural leader of the crew and most ambitious, seems to have all the answers.

'Where would you live?' Elias asks Saib.

'Have you ever heard of Yusuf?' He asks refusing Elias a chance to answer.

'He migrated to Australia decades ago, leaving his village a very poor man. Remarkably he built an incredible fortune in Australia, all from hard work and clever investments. You should see how much property he owns now; we can only dream of it but it's there for the taking. How hungry are you, Elias?'

'Very.' Elias asserts. 'How do we get in touch with him? Will he help us?'

'For a price.' Saib insists. 'He worked hard to make his fortune, and if he helps others, he wants to be rewarded somehow.'

'Not just to help his people?' Elias asks naively.

Saib laughs, as do the rest of the crew.

'How do you think he got this rich? You need to learn to be shrewd my friend.' Saib smirks.

'What's so special about this man?' Elias asks, not sold.

'Over the years Yusuf has made lots of important friends in the business community in Australia, bank managers, landlords, real estate agents, factory owners and so on. With every new piece of property, he purchased over the years, the business ties grew stronger. Being a clever man Yusuf could see a business opportunity before anyone else. He watched with a keen eye the rise in migration of young men out of Lebanon into Australia, he saw that he could benefit from it. Using his business contacts, Yusuf knew he could arrange work and a place to stay for the migrant men on arrival to Australia. He would eventually help with organising bank loans to buy property if they wanted to invest. All his contacts would benefit, factory owners from the influx of unskilled labour, real estate agents from successful leasing of accom-modation and bank managers for arranging home loans to migrants desperate to buy a home, in that way they received commission.'

'How does Yusuf benefit so much?' Elias asks, but the work crew roar with laughter at him.

'Yusuf benefits the most, all he has to do is help men like us journey across to the land of opportunity, we need work and accommodation, and he sets it up for us, but for a price. He then gets money from his business contacts every time he supplies them with labour, tenants and so on.' Saib explains.

Not surprisingly, Yusuf quickly becomes the go to man for all eager young men wanting to migrate to Australia. Elias can see how Yusuf will be instrumental in his plan to escape from here, the key to migrating to a country with endless opportunities. Regardless of Nadeem's objections Elias remains resolute in going ahead with his plan to migrate. He continues to pocket a portion of his wages and gradually saves for his passage to Australia.

The closer Elias gets to paying for his passage the more he and Leila fight over his decision. Although Nadeem knows nothing of his plans, Elias has confided in his mother. Today he regrets this because Leila won't stop begging him to change his mind.

'Your father won't allow it.' Leila cries.

'I don't care what he thinks? He doesn't want me to go because he's afraid I'll build my own wealth, that would crush him, of course he will try and stop me.' He insists.

'I don't want you to go son, please I can't live without you.' She begs.

'I have stayed long enough, I can't bare it any longer, you wouldn't let me go before but now I'm old enough. I can't stand his criticism; it destroys any confidence I have.'

He stares helplessly at his mother hoping she will understand. Leila does understand but she can't bear the thought of him leaving. Elias is frustrated and distraught and won't budge this time.

'If I go to Australia, I can make a lot of money, I have heard so many stories like this. It's the only chance our family will have to be spared from a life of poverty. I know that if my father was alive, he would support me, because this would guarantee our family a good life.'

'Stop, stop. Your father would have wanted to keep the family together, not drive us a world apart.' She insists.

I'll send for the whole family to come once I have saved enough money, I promise.'

'You are breaking my heart son.' Leila cries.

'I'm going mother.' His mind is made up.

Using her apron to dry tears Leila stares sadly at Elias.

'I can't change your mind, even if this is breaking my heart, I can't stop you.' She hesitates before continuing, nervous about what she needs to tell him. 'The only way he'll let you go is if you take Charbel.'

Elias suddenly goes red in the face, overcome with rage.

'Never.' He snaps.

'Please don't cause trouble, you know what he is like.' She begs out of fear.

'I won't do it. He can't make me.'

'I don't want either of you to go. I want my sons here with their family. This will kill me.' The tears begin to flow again.

'He said he didn't want me to go, because of the shop. Why is it suddenly ok for both of us to go?'

'He knew you would go anyway, so he thought it would be safer for both of you to travel together.'

'That's not true, he could not care less about me. He just doesn't want me to succeed. If Charbel succeeds as well, he won't feel so bad, his own flesh and blood doing as well as me will contain his jealousy. Why does he hate me so much? And who will pay for Charbel's passage to Australia?' Elias demands.

'Your father has some savings.' She explains aware of the injustice, Elias worked so hard to save for his passage.

He paces up and down the kitchen and then stops in his tracks, raging with anger.

'I'll show him. I will work harder than I ever have, and I will become rich. I will prove to him that I am far better than his son.'

'Of course, you will be successful son.' She tries to calm him. 'You are so determined but remember that family will always be much more important than wealth, power, any of those things. Be kind to your brother, he loves you and would never harm you. Don't make him pay for all the wrongdoings of his father.' Leila insists.

And so, Elias is forced to abandon his friends who plan to leave for Australia in a month, he will instead travel with his brother a couple of months later when Nadeem can release Charbel from the store. Nadeem asks his father to help in Charbel's place, a humiliating prospect for the retiree, but he has no choice but to say yes. The impact of the depression has been so bad that working for his son is necessary to afford the essentials. The tide has turned for this once wealthy family and Nadeem has placed his hope in Charbel to turn that around again.

4

The Voyage

In the winter of 1946 Elias and Charbel embark on a journey halfway across the world, destined for Australia the foreign continent which will soon become their new home. Charbel departs unwillingly, feeling pressured into going by his father, the constant badgering has pushed him to concede and reluctantly leave behind the country and family he loves. By nature, Charbel is not adventurous nor ambitious like his older brother, and this has gnawed away at Nadeem for years. The younger brother finds his impending voyage terrifying, all the while dreading the thought of leaving behind his mother and sisters whom he adores, missing his father to a lesser extent. The village and all its people make up the world he knows and loves, and now he is forced to leave it all behind. Charbel has suffered many sleepless nights of late, worrying constantly about how his brother might treat him on their voyage over the long months ahead. He is aware of the adverse effect his father has had on their relationship, what should be a strong bond between two brothers is the opposite. Elias has resented Charbel since he was small, watching his brother grow up as the favoured son filled him with jealousy and rage. Charbel, on the other hand has always adored his older brother, but he understands why Elias struggles to feel the same way.

On the eve of Elias and Charbel's departure, the entire village congregate in the town centre to bid the brother's farewell. They gather to celebrate and mourn the departure of these two courageous young men who are about to embark on their passage to Australia. They are saddened by their loss of two well respected members of the community whom they will miss dearly. Nevertheless, the community celebrate the prospect of wealth and a better life that awaits the brothers. More to the point, they want to remind the boys not to forget the ones they leave behind, anticipating the brothers will share their good fortune, the church will expect regular donations from them once they find work. The community revel in the possibility that the brothers may pave the way for others in their village to follow. Unlike Elias's adventurous workmates, not many from their village have gone to Australia for a new life. And so, the villagers will wait to see how Elias and Charbel do first. Despite the poverty that plagues them, the community are unwilling to leave just yet. They will only follow in the boys' footsteps if the prosperity Australia claims to offer is guaranteed.

The departure is most heartbreaking for Leila who can't bear the thought of her sons leaving for a foreign land, especially not knowing when she'll see them again. Endless tears and heartache will torment her every single day and not until she sees them again will Leila have peace of mind.

She swallows back the tears for now, because tonight the community wish to honour the brothers with a celebration for their courageous act, hoping they will pave the way for more of them to follow. They hope this will be the beginning of many opportunities for the younger members of the community, allowing them a chance to build prosperous lives abroad where poverty has no place.

The next morning is a tough one for the brothers, their mother hasn't stopped crying and has been stalling their departure. Filled with dread she finally gives in and lets them go. Leila watches her sons finally board their taxi, by now the driver has grown impatient with her many attempts to delay their inevitable goodbye. As the taxi pulls away Leila cries inconsolably wondering when or if she'll see her sons again.

Their journey starts with a long taxi ride to Haifa where the brothers spend two nights in a hotel. This proves to be an adventure of a lifetime for Elias because he has never stayed in a hotel before, let alone in a big city. Nadeem has taken them on the occasional drive to Beirut and Tripoli but never to stay, just a day trip. Elias is thrilled to be getting further and further away from his stepfather, although, like his brother, he misses his mother and sisters already. Unsurprisingly Charbel does not share the same sense of adventure as his brother, instead he tries to bury deep his feelings of sadness and homesickness, not an easy feat. He is completely out of his comfort zone which makes him very nervous and even slightly depressed.

From Haifa they travel to Egypt by train, along the Suez Canal. They watch the waterway pass as their train speeds along, oblivious to its purpose. How would they know it was a route of trade between Europe and Asia, their education was limited to the history of Lebanon, and mainly their village. Staring out of the window, the brothers are amazed by how fast the train travels, they have never travelled like this before.

On arrival to Egypt, they suddenly feel overwhelmed by the large crowds, never have they seen this many people, not even in Beirut. Charbel latches on tightly to his brother's arm, surprisingly Elias doesn't pull away from him, he can see the terror in his younger brothers' eyes. Although slightly nervous, Elias isn't scared, he wants to take it all in, he feels exhilarated and charged with excitement at the site of this large foreign city. He can feel the thrill of adventure flowing through his veins, and for the first time he doesn't feel the controlling grip of his father, something that has held him back for far too many years. Later that day they board their ship in Cairo and set sail for Australia, the 'New World' a term coined by the many migrants that settled there around this time.

A few days into their passage the adventure begins to wane, the vessel is not what they imagined it to be. As it happens their ship is far from comfortable, the boat had been purpose built to carry soldiers during the second world war and was only recently converted to accommodate post war migration. Even worse, the brothers find themselves bunking in a dormitory of hundreds of passengers, something they did not anticipate. Most disappointingly, the brothers find the foreign food unpalatable, and they already begin to miss their mother's delicious cooking. The bread isn't flat like what they are used to, condiments and sauces are used to cook with rather than the fresh spices, garlic, and onion. Worst of all they don't use any olive oil to cook with or add to salads. The servings of meats are too big and the vegetables and salads too meagre. The selection of food is not only unpleasant to eat but it also wreaks havoc on their stomachs, leading to numerous trips to the toilet and sometimes no visits when the food sits in their gut for days. Still, they have no choice but to eat this strange food or else go hungry.

The foreign food makes Charbel's home sickness worse, he barely eats, and Elias starts to worry. Not only does Charbel miss his mother's cooking, but the strange languages passengers speak adds to his sense of loneliness. Elias doesn't like the food, nor does he tolerate the language barrier, but he distracts himself by focussing on what the future holds for him. Even so, he feels bad for his younger brother which surprises him, all he has ever felt for his brother is resentment and envy.

One day Elias decides he must do something about Charbel because he isn't eating and looks depressed most of the time. He finds his way to the galley hoping to gather some food at least similar to what they are used to. He walks into the kitchen and approaches a tall overweight and dishevelled looking cook who is bursting at the seams in his under-sized chef's uniform.

'What do you want?' The chef snaps at Elias in English. 'Dinner isn't served for another two hours.'

Elias stares blankly at the chef because he doesn't speak or understand a word of English.

'Get lost idiot, it's not time to eat.' The chef mutters in French.

But this time Elias understands, French is his second language, a mandatory subject at school in Lebanon at the time. Ignoring the chef's rudeness Elias sees this as an opportunity to communicate with him and hopefully get what he needs.

'True, I don't speak English, but my French is very good.' Elias smiles at the chef speaking in fluent French. The chef goes red in the face, embarrassed by his rudeness.

'Yes, your French is very good.' He admits sheepishly. 'Sorry, I didn't mean to insult you, but I'm turning people away all day because they don't know what time the kitchen opens, they can't read the signs?' He rambles off in French.

'It's ok, maybe you can help me.' Elias smiles cunningly, having picked up some of the shrewd antics his workmates taught him.

'I hate to trouble you because I know you are very busy, but you see my brother hasn't eaten in days. He finds this food very strange, he is not used to it and won't eat, I'm very worried about him.'

'You are not alone, most passengers have the same problem, but I can only cook with what they supply.' It's all we serve, I'm sorry.' The chef explains.

Elias smiles at him and then pulls out a bottle of clear liquor and hands it to the chef.

'It's arak, home distilled and fifty per cent pure alcohol. Are you sure there's nothing else you can make for my brother?' Elias smiles.

'This looks strong.' The chef grins as he grabs the bottle from Elias.

'My mother cooks lovely Lebanese dishes all the time and sometimes I took time to watch her. I have some idea about what ingredients to use.' Elias smiles as he pulls a notebook from his bag. 'Also, she wrote these recipes down for me, somehow she must have known the food would be different.'

The chef takes the notebook, looks at it and laughs. 'This is in Arabic; I can't read it.' Shaking his head.

'That's ok, I'll read it out for you, better still I'll write some in French. The Kibbeh is the easiest so we can start with that.' Elias smiles.

'I have no idea what kibbeh is, and have you seen what there is in the storage and cool-room?' The chef laughs.

'Do you have meat?' Elias asks.

'Well, yes of course.' He admits.

'Salt, pepper and garlic?' Elias enquires

'Only salt and pepper.' He replies.

Elias pulls out a plastic bag of cracked wheat, bottled spices and a head of garlic from his bag and hands them to the chef. The chef smiles and allows Elias into his tiny kitchen.

'My mother demanded I take all of this on our journey, she was worried we would die of starvation if there was no Lebanese food to eat.' They both laugh at how silly that sounds but then Elias stops, suddenly struck by the sobering thought that his mother was genuinely terrified that her sons might starve. The fear of starvation has plagued her for years, it took an entire family from her, bar her precious son.

They are weeks into their travels when Charbel's homesickness begins to lift, thanks in part to his brother's connections with the chef. Elias convinces the chef to get creative with his cuisines and he agrees, but on the condition the bag of spices and recipes stay in his kitchen, at least for the duration of the voyage. Elias obliges, he couldn't possibly go back to eating the rot that had been served up. He strikes a deal with the chef, suggesting they split the profits if Elias manages to sell the left-over meals after hours, to those who miss a meal or want second helpings. Everyday Elias becomes more obsessed with conjuring up plans on how to make money, showing strong signs of an astute businessman in the making, his workmates certainly rubbed off on him. Moreover, Elias is well-liked by people, over the years he has developed an ability to get on very well with people, especially customers and he hopes to use this skill to his advantage in time, when he eventually opens a store of his own.

Elias has become very supportive of his brother throughout his bouts of homesickness, often staying up half the night with him, lending an ear when Charbel struggled to sleep. The brothers have begun to take English classes together on the boat, they go along each morning arriving early because the room fills up quickly. The classroom is tiny, spilling over with students hoping to speak a little English before reaching their new homeland. They know that speaking some English on arrival to the new world will help them find work and hopefully build a good life. The brothers are surprised by how quickly they are picking up the language.

Just as they begin to settle into their passage rough seas form, forcing powerful waves to crash against their ship for days on end. This terrifies the brothers who have never experienced anything like this before. Most passengers suffer extreme motion sickness leaving a constant smell of vomit, especially in the corridors. The dining rooms empty out because no one can stomach food, this is disappointing for Elias who was profiting from selling leftover food. To get some fresh air and relief from the smell of vomit the brothers head up onto the deck, but they don't last long up there fearing the gale force winds. It's not just the wind that scares them, but also the crashing waves and torrential rain. And so, they are forced back to their room where they wait out the storm. When they can't sleep at night the brothers pray earnestly hoping not to perish at sea.

When the rough seas finally settle the brothers rejoice, praising God for sparing their lives, but the relief is short-lived. What follows is the sight of endless stretches of sea with no land in sight, week after week all they see is water and they yearn for the sight of a coastline that seems a million years away. The brothers sit idly on deck gazing at the boundless deep blue sea that goes on and on, and they can't help but think about home.

'Do you miss home?' Charbel asks his brother.

'Of course, I do, who wouldn't?'

'I miss our family, and I can't stop thinking about mother's cooking, in fact I miss everything about home.' Charbel gets emotional.

'I know how you feel, it's hard. But we must keep focussed on the future, the opportunities that lay ahead. I try not to think too much about today, tomorrow, or next week. Instead, my eyes are on next month, next year and the years and decades that follow. If we work hard and save, we will be rich beyond our dreams.' Elias gushes with excitement.

'I don't care about that, it's not important to me. I just want to have enough, that's all, and I could have had that back in our village.' He says solemnly. 'I do try to focus on the future but it's hard to do when all I can think about is what I have left behind.' He stares sadly into the horizon as they edge further away from home.

'Try not to think too much about it and before too long, our whole family will be with us in Australia. Be patient brother, stay focussed and work hard.' Elias smiles warmly at his brother, Charbel forces a smile back, knowing his brother's heart is in the right place.

'If you save enough money in Australia, you can buy your own house in the village. That way you can go back to the village every year in the summer and stay in your own house. You'll enjoy the delicious food of our country, not what they feed us now. You can visit all the people you've missed and go to the local church every day, just like we have always done. When you go back everyone will look up to you for what you have achieved.' Elias smiles at his brother but Charbel is unconvinced.

'I could have had all that if I stayed behind and I don't care about who looks up to me.' Charbel insists.

'What about our family? The cost of living is rising every day and it will only get worse.' Elias insists. 'What you would save in our village over ten years, you could make in under a year where we are going.' He says hoping Charbel will see sense.

'You're right, but it doesn't take away the terrible homesickness, but I'll try not to think about it, just like you say.' Charbel says solemnly.

Since leaving the village Elias and Charbel have formed a strong bond, without Nadeem around there is nobody to drive them apart. The resentment towards Charbel no longer festers, Elias has grown fond of his little brother, and this makes him feel good. He misses his mother terribly but tries hard to bury those thoughts deeply. He is determined not to be derailed by anything that might throw him off his pathway to success.

Months into their passage and Charbel hasn't missed a single English class since joining. Unbeknownst to Elias, his motivation is not purely driven by a determination to learn English, in fact he mainly goes because he wants to spend time with a pretty student called Hilda, she caught his eye the very first day they met. Hilda is a strikingly beautiful Lithuanian woman in her early twenties. and she has also fallen for Charbel. He is entranced by her long locks of golden blond hair, milky white skin, and light blue eyes, she is all he can think about, and she feels the same way about him. The two lovebirds are inseparable in class and while they struggle to communicate in English their eyes speak volumes about how they feel for one another. Like all the other students they are eager to learn English in a hurry, but for them it's so they can understand one another better.

Elias watches this relationship blossom with great trepidation knowing Nadeem would be enraged if he found out, likely to blame Elias for it. Although Nadeem's family has lost all their wealth, they still have a good reputation to uphold. The family would not want to give the village community any reason to question their standing amongst them. Charbel falling in love with a non-Lebanese woman would be judged harshly, bringing the family name into disrepute. Elias refrains from saying anything for now, hoping the relationship will fizzle out as soon as they arrive in Australia when they will be forced to go their separate ways.

One night during a bad storm the brothers struggle to sleep. They lay awake nervously awaiting the bad weather to pass. The seas are rough, much worse than they have been before and it's hard to distract from worry.

'The storm is getting worse; those waves are crashing hard.' Charbel insists in a panicked state.

It will pass, just like all the other storms have done.' Elias tries to calm his brother.

'I hope so.' Charbel sighs nervously.

'Keep your mind off the storm, think about something nice and the time will pass quickly, before you know it the rough seas will weaken into calmer waters, it always does.' He says reassuringly.

As Charbel tries to think happy thoughts the first thing that comes to mind is Hilda and he smiles to himself. He would love to tell Elias all about her, to be able to share the joys of their budding romance. But the reality is he can't, aware of how his brother would react, so he doesn't say a word.

'I know you are thinking about something, what is it?' Elias prods, and Charbel hesitates.

'Come on?' Elias insists impatiently.

'It will make you angry so don't ask.' Charbel sighs. With that Elias bottles up, suddenly wishing he never said anything.

The brothers fall silent and after a while the quietness is unbearable. Charbel wrestles with the thought of telling him and finally decides to come clean.

'I'm in love, I have never felt this way before.' He hesitates before continuing but his brothers cold silence does not make it easy. 'She is the most beautiful girl I have ever seen.' He insists, hoping and praying his brother will understand.

Elias moans, very annoyed by his brother's infatuation.

'Please say something?' Charbel begs, the silence is unbearable.

'What should I say?' Elias finally snaps. 'Do you want me to celebrate this ridiculous behaviour?'

'It's not ridiculous, Hilda is a lovely woman. She's so kind and warm, why judge so harshly when you don't even know her?'

'Stop it.' Elias shouts. 'This woman is not Lebanese; she is not one of us. What do you think your father would say? What about our reputation, the shame you will bring onto your entire family?' Elias seethes.

'How would they ever know?' Charbel protests. 'When we are all together as one family again, I will obey their customs. I will marry in accordance with tradition, but for now I want to enjoy this beautiful friendship while it lasts, because it brings me so much joy.'

'I think you are playing with fire. You don't just stay friends with someone you have feelings for. Be careful Charbel, I think you are making a mistake, but I have said enough.' Elias sighs and their conversation ends as the storm settles into silence.

5

The New World

After four long months at sea their voyage finally comes to an end, Elias and Charbel reach the shores of Australia, the new world awaits them. They arrive in the winter months and are surprised by how mild the temperature is, such a sharp contrast to the freezing cold winters in their village nestled high in the mountains. It hits them hard how far they have travelled, to be on opposite sides of the world where it's winter here and back home the village begins to welcome the warm summer months. This foreign and faraway land will become their new home, which fills Elias with excitement and Charbel with terrible bouts of homesickness. Elias still misses his family and beloved Lebanon, but he is adamant that this will become his new home. He refuses to get emotional about his family and home in Lebanon and focusses on what lies ahead. He is charged with excitement knowing the 'lucky country' offers him so many opportunities and a welcome distance from his stepfather. Unlike his brother, Charbel has little interest in wealth, rather he delights in the prospect of pursuing his blossoming relationship with Hilda. He must now hide his burgeoning love for Hilda because Elias will certainly have something to say about it. When it came down to it, Charbel couldn't walk away from Hilda at the end of their journey, this broken promise will infuriate Elias but leaving her would have broken Charbel's heart.

In line with the deal they made with Yusuf before leaving Lebanon, the brothers are set up with work and a place to stay when they first arrive in the country. Although they appreciate the helpful start Yusuf provides, the way he runs his operation does not sit well with them. They are expected to work extremely long days but only get paid for eight hours, and their accommodation is worse than what it was on the boat. The boarding house they stay in is crowded with tiny bedrooms and a communal bathroom and kitchen and is terribly unkept without out the domestic help of a cleaner. None of these men even know how to clean, having relied on their mothers or wives to take care of that kind of thing.

The dwelling spills over with migrant men all lured to the new world for a better life, all expected to work the same long hours as Elias and Charbel. Yusuf profits handsomely from this arrangement and has no plans to soften the deal. The brothers decide very early on that this will not do, but for now they must work hard and put up with the substandard lodgings until they can afford to move someplace else. Elias has already tried to locate some of his old workmates from back home, they would surely have moved on by now having arrived months earlier.

The upside to this living arrangement is that the brothers end up making lots of new friends. Just like Elias and Charbel, the residents are new migrants from not just Lebanon but also Italy, Greece, Malta as well as other countries impacted by the war. Together they all form a close bond from shared experiences, the yearning for family and the homeland they left behind in pursuit of a better life. To help cope with their homesickness they come together each night after work and often talk about all those they left behind. They also practice their English in the evenings which makes for lots of laughs, the pronunciation and inflexion of their language's contrasts sharply with the slow Aussie twang. The expressive and emotional tone of an Italian saying 'mate-tah' instead of 'mate' has them all in stitches and it's not just the Italian's pronunciation that sounds funny, it's the same for all of them. Nobody takes offence, they all laugh seeing the humour in it.

By virtue of their different cultures the kitchen becomes a melting pot of culinary delights from all around the world and the men enjoy their nightly feasts. Each night they take turns and try to cook dishes from their own country, some of the dishes come off nicely and others not so much. Most of these men have been spoilt by their mothers who have prepared food for them since they were babies. Over time the living arrangement temper their homesickness, but after six months of lots of laughter and camaraderie Elias and Charbel decide it's time to find a new home.

As Yusuf has packaged their deal to include work and accommodation there is no choice in taking one or the other, it must be both, otherwise Yusuf loses a slice of his profit, something he is unwilling to do. And so, the brothers seek out better paid work which is not hard to do during a post-war era whereby Australia has a chronic shortage of unskilled labour.

Their new job certainly pays well but it is backbreaking work, and the hours are very long, even so that does little to discourage the brothers who are used to that. They pick up another job that they work during the evening, but Charbel does not keep that up for long; and Elias ends up taking a third job on the weekends. With all that hard work they can afford to move into a flat of their own, finally a private bathroom and kitchen, they have shared those facilities for ten months so are overjoyed to leave that all behind. Even with the extra money, Elias insists on a one-bedroom flat, he wants to keep rental cost down so they can save to buy a house.

Months pass and Elias continues to buckle down working day and night, and weekends, he barely has time to sleep. Both brothers work in construction as labourers during the day, spending long hours paving asphalt roads under the hot summer sun. Charbel gave up his second job after only a month, deciding labouring day and night just wasn't worth it. The job pays well, but Charbel has never wanted to build a fortune like his brother. Rather than work all the time and save extra money, Charbel spends lots of time with Hilda going out to the movies and nice restaurants, and with Elias at work he has been able to get away with it.

Spending evenings together is not enough for Charbel and Hilda, they long to be together all the time, so when Hilda tells him she has managed to get him a job at the factory she works at, he is overjoyed. The job is with a textile manufacturer, and it pays far better than his day job paving roads. Hilda confesses the work is automated and mundane but there are fixed start and finish times with set break times which managers can't change. This is thanks to the trade union that protects worker rights, something Charbel has never heard about. The worker pays a union fee, a small cost, which is automatically deducted from their pay and in doing so they receive protection from their union organiser or representative. If an employer tries to exploit any worker that belongs to a union the representative quickly challenges their actions and the employer backs away.

In sharp contrast, the brothers are worked to the bone without a set start and finish time. They begin their day before sunrise and finish late into the evening, sometimes without a break. It's no surprise then that Charbel is delighted to accept the job, and he doesn't hesitate about his decision to work at the factory. There is no such union for the building and construction workers to sign up to at the time, so the poor road crew work hard, under extremely unfair and harsh working conditions.

When Charbel tells Elias about his new job he makes certain not to mention that Hilda works there, he continues to keep this secret even though he hates lying to his brother, but he has no other choice. He tells Elias he simply can't keep working under such harsh conditions, working outdoors under the relentless heat of the Australian summer months is something he'll never get used to. It's so different to the comfortable summers spent in their village perched high in the mountains of Lebanon. Elias thinks nothing of it, he is far too focussed on building his wealth to be bothered by unnecessary distractions like this, in fact he's happy because it only affirms that he is far stronger than his little brother, his only regret being that Nadeem is not here to see it.

And so, now Charbel and Hilda can spend more time together and their burgeoning love affair flourishes, but sadly it will all be at a cost in time. Charbel knows deep down that he will never be permitted to marry Hilda, it is forbidden to wed outside of their culture and race. He can't bear to think about leaving Hilda for now, his family won't be here for some time so he buries his head in the sand pretending all will be fine.

In 1948 the brothers are still living in their tiny inner city flat nearby

Redfern, it has been two years since they moved but Elias refuses to get a bigger place, unwilling to pay higher rent. Although they reluctantly share their home with unwelcome cockroaches and an occasional rat, at least their bathroom and kitchen are private. Nevertheless, by enduring less than favourable living conditions those sacrifices have meant they have been able to save rather than squander their money on expensive rent, Elias often reminds Charbel. The sacrifice has paid off though, because now they have a large deposit to go towards purchasing a house.

The next challenge for the brothers is navigating through the complicated home loan application process, whilst they can speak English well enough their ability to read and write needs improvement. Wading through the detailed forms given to them by the bank manager is stressful, they don't understand much of it at all. Calling on Yusuf for help is the only way, but they fear he will not assist after breaking the deal agreed upon prior to leaving Lebanon, they wonder if seeking out new jobs and accommodation might not have been such a great idea after all.

Surprisingly Yusuf doesn't hold a grudge, instead he happily helps them complete all the forms needed for the loan application. When the loan is finally approved the brothers can't believe it, they are so excited to be buying a house. Not long after the loan approval they hear through the grapevine that Yusuf received handsome commission from the bank for bringing in new business, each time he brings new customer to the bank, he benefits. Rather than criticise Yusuf for his greed, Elias aspires to be more like him, he wants to become a shrewd and astute businessman as well.

When the brothers finally purchase their three-bedroom house it feels surreal, this would never have been possible had they stayed in Lebanon. They write to the family back home sharing the good news and prompting them to start preparing for their impending move to Australia.

Since arriving in Australia, the brothers have struggled to find food that is remotely like the culinary delights enjoyed back home. It has been impossible to find any stores that sell Lebanese food or stock the ingredients needed to cook with. There are not enough established Lebanese businesspeople in the country yet to run stores like this. Furthermore, there is insufficient demand from Lebanese migrants to buy food from these stores, not yet. Without high demand from customers, it won't be a profitable business venture, if it was, Yusuf would have already done it.

Nevertheless, just recently Elias has discovered a nearby grocer in Redfern that sells ingredients similar the ones his mother uses to cook with, but they would need to cook the food which won't be such an easy feat. Unfortunately, their cooking skills have not improved much at all since their time in the boarding house. Up until now they have been eating homemade sandwiches, and take away food, it has been too long since they enjoyed a good home cooked Lebanese meal. So, they eagerly go to the store and buy up all the ingredients to cook with, but it doesn't end well, most of the food burns to a crisp and ends up in the bin. The brothers are disheartened by their failed attempt to cook the Lebanese dishes and end up feeling terribly homesick for their mothers cooking. Equally as upsetting for Elias is having to throw away food, he cringes at the thought of wasting money, so he tries hard to salvage some of the burnt lamb Charbel threw into the bin. He cuts away the burnt edges on the meat and makes sandwiches, so he has lunch covered for the rest of the week, this cheers him up somewhat. Fortunately, a Lebanese restaurant is about to open on Cleveland Street and Charbel can't wait, Elias isn't too keen because he doesn't want to waste his money, but he longs for Lebanese food and will pay for it.

Over the past two years Elias has not strayed once from his plan to build his fortunes and he has worked day and night every day of the week to edge closer to that goal. Even so, on Sunday he starts his working day later because he won't miss church, surprisingly not even for money. Charbel on the other hand only works at the textile factory which frees him up to enjoy time with Hilda, although he still manages to save ample because the factory pays well. Unlike his brother, Charbel only works as hard as he needs to, if he can pay for necessities and some luxuries, he's happy. Despite not working ridiculous hours like Elias, he still makes an equal contribution to their newly purchased house, the home that the entire family will eventually reside in. He works to pay his share of the rent, cover the cost of food and of course spoil Hilda with fun evenings out, but he doesn't want for anything more. Elias doesn't care that Charbel lacks ambition to build wealth, in fact it makes him proud to know that Nadeem's son by birth will never be as successful as him.

What does enrage Elias is his little brother's unwillingness to stop seeing Hilda, he recently caught Charbel out with Hilda during a rare night out to the city with his workmates. A week ago, Elias reluctantly joined his workmates for a night out in the city, curious to see what all the fuss was about. He surprisingly enjoyed himself, but the joy faded the moment he saw Charbel and Hilda. He thought that their relationship had ended a few years ago, so was livid by the discovery and hurt by his brother's deception. Naturally fierce arguments have ensued since then, but Charbel refuses to leave Hilda no matter what his brother says, he will only end the relationship once the rest of the family migrate to Australia. Elias shakes his head in disbelief wondering why his brother is being so foolish, but he backs off hoping Charbel follows through with his promise this time.

A few weeks later when things have settled a little between the two, Charbel manages to talk his brother into going to a dance with him, pleading that this will be their last chance to have some real fun before the family's imminent arrival. Elias knows that when Nadeem arrives there will be no such freedom, and up until now he hasn't had much fun at all, certainly not like his little brother. He knows there will be beautiful young ladies at the dance tonight and ponders over the thought of dancing closely with one or even two of them. For a moment he feels carefree, yearning to have some fun, but that sadly fades as he struggles to shake off the thought of what his stepfather might say about it. The nagging thought of Nadeem judging his every move makes it hard to relax and have any fun. Unknowingly, Elias has become more like Nadeem since arriving in the country, he now holds extremely traditional views and has become very judgmental, He has become obsessed by what his stepfather will think. And so, sadly he can't ignore how the night out might be perceived by others, fearing that if anyone from their community ever found out they were fraternising with women like this, then that could cast shame on their family name.

With that Elias decides this is not worth it, he sinks into the couch in his tailored suit and lights a cigarette appearing to settle in for the night. Charbel notices and sighs in frustration.

'They're all waiting for us at the dance hall, why are you taking your time?' Charbel snaps, annoyed by his brother's stubbornness.

'They can wait, we still have time.' Elias continues to delay.

'They want to see you, all of Hilda's friends are excited to meet you.' He pushes but Elias doesn't care, rather he gets annoyed.

'These girls are Latvian?' Elias snaps. 'What do you think our parents will say? You know they will disapprove but you keep going out with her. Why haven't you ended this relationship?' Elias demands to know.

Charbel looks shocked by his brother's sudden change in mood and hurt by what he thinks of Hilda.

'I love her.' Charbel insists.

'You are a fool, stop acting like this.' Elias chastises.

'I am in love with her, but you can't understand.' Charbel looks hurt.

'Well, you will have to leave her eventually, and the longer you stay with her the harder it will be to let go. He will beat you up for being with this woman, don't you understand?' Elias tries to protect his brother.

'I know that, but I will worry about it when our family gets here.' Charbel sighs.

'Then go out, but don't expect me to support this kind of behaviour. It's unacceptable and if anyone from our village ever found out, it would certainly bring shame on us, our family name. I'm tired and have work in the morning, so go without me.' Elias says, annoyed by Charbel's defiance.

'Brother, you work seven days a week from early morning to late at night, when will you stop? When will there be enough money for you? We have already saved hard to buy a house for all the family when they come. How much more do you need?' Charbel insists.

'Are you stupid? In Lebanon we were struggling like poor people, here you can build a fortune through hard work. Who would not want to work hard? You don't know how lucky you are.' Elias shakes his head in disbelief.

'We already live well, once we move into our house, we will be very comfortable, what are you trying to do to yourself?'

'What does it matter to you?' Elias snaps again.

'Because I want you to be happy!' Charbel insists.

'Our mother nearly died during the famine because there was no money to buy food on the black market. My father did die, along with the rest of the family. I never want to be poor.' Elias stares ruthlessly at his brother.

'I understand brother, but we have plenty now, we will never starve.' Charbel insists empathetically.

Elias shakes his head staring at Charbel with vengeance.

'For you, what has been accomplished so far is enough. For me, in the eyes of your father, not enough has been done. In his eyes, you have been perfect from the day you were born. But not so for me, I am never good enough. But I will show him, very soon I'll have my own grocery store, one far better than the one he had.'

'I am not him.' Charbel shouts at his brother in frustration, and Elias looks taken back by the uncharacteristic outburst, Charbel is always calm and measured. He takes a deep breath instantly regretting his actions.

'What I want for you comes from my heart, I want you to be happy.' Charbel stares compassionately at his brother.

Elias stares remorsefully at his brother, regretting taking aim at an innocent bystander. It's Nadeem that he despises but it's Charbel he has attacked. Sadly, Elias is too proud to explain this to his brother and shuts the door closed on any prospect of talking it through.

'Just be quiet when you come home, I have work in the morning and need a good night's sleep.' With that Elias ends their conversation. Charbel leaves the room closing the door quietly behind him.

Two years on and the rest of the family have yet to move to Australia, but they will be arriving soon. Heartbroken, Leila has cried every day since the day her sons left her. Nadeem struggles to find a buyer for the store and grows increasingly nervous that he won't have enough money to move his family to Australia, so many from the village have already left. He is desperate to marry off his daughters who are getting older and wonders how he will ever be able to do that without enough money to bargain with. Elias and Charbel have offered to help the family with the cost of their journey, but Nadeem is too proud to accept, as the patriarch he must pay.

The boys miss their family terribly but carry on with their lives hoping and praying it won't be too much longer before they arrive. Charbel spends all his free time with Hilda, which continues to infuriate Elias. He tries to focus on his goals rather his younger brother's antics, and so he keeps working long hours. The hard work has paid off for him, at least that's what he tells himself. Elias beams with pride at his latest acquisition, the purchase of a mixed business grocery store. With his sharpened business sense, unconsciously driven by a constant need to prove himself to Nadeem, Elias manages to negotiate a good price for the store. Nothing brings him more pleasure than knowing his wealth continues to grow and buying the shop has brought him closer to that goal. The store trades seven days a week, and he opens very early in the morning and closes late at night. On Sunday he starts a little later so he can attend mass, but as soon as the closing prayers end, he springs to his feet and hurries off to open the shop.

Elias is very proud of his store, fitting it out himself to save money of course. Any opportunity to save and Elias has his hand in it. He has built the shelving for his store using old wooden crates that some wholesaler at the fruit and vegetable market threw away. Proudly resourceful Elias simply sanded back the wood adding two fresh coats of white paint and built his shelving. He can't understand the mentality of the Australian people, why they discard and waste so much, but he just takes advantage of their wasteful habits. He can't believe that every three months the local council picks up 'junk' from the front of residential homes. He doesn't understand why these people throw away valuable goods like furniture and the like, items that could be salvaged. On the night before council pick up Elias takes his ute out for a drive and sorts threw a goldmine of garbage. He manages to pick up enough good quality furniture to fit out the house they will soon move into.

Although he considers the Australian people spoilt in comparison to how they live back in the village, he can't resist indulging in some of their delicacies. When it comes to stocking his shop Elias can't believe the wide selection of food, he is able source from the wholesaler. There are so many different assortments of food, a large variety of breakfast cereals, coffee and tea, pasta, rice, tins of spam ham and even different types of olive oil. Elias delights in being able to sell just about anything he wants in his store. And so, he stocks groceries including fruit and vegetables, hot pies and sausage rolls and a whole variety of freshly made sandwiches which he prepares daily. He has even annexed a milk bar with a fancy milkshake maker which is becoming very popular.

Running a mixed business means life is very busy for Elias. He operates the store and stocks it mainly on his own, Charbel helps after work when he can. Every Monday morning Elias gets up before dawn to make his way to the markets and buy fruit and vegetables for the shop, he needs to do this before the store opens. To stock his shop with perishable and non-perishable foods he also takes a trip to the wholesaler every Tuesday and Thursday afternoon. Elias can't trust anybody other than his brother to cover the afternoons when he must go to the wholesalers, like Nadeem he worries they might dip their hand into the till. Charbel works at the factory six days a week and starts at 6am each day so he can't help in the mornings but helps his brother every Tuesday and Thursday afternoon. Although Charbel doesn't understand his brother's obsession with money, he wants Elias to be happy and if money does that, so be it.

Through very long hours of work both brothers have paid off the house they purchased for the family, and they eagerly look forward to their arrival which is in just over a month. They received word a month ago through the mail that their father had sold the general store which has paid for the family's passage to Australia and to expect them in the coming months. Elias is nervous about seeing his stepfather, life has been very peaceful and pleasant without him around, and the brothers have grown much closer away from his meddling ways. However, with the years apart from Nadeem, Elias has forgotten just how badly his stepfather had treated him. He foolishly thinks that perhaps it won't be so bad having Nadeem around to help him in his shop. More trusted labour at his fingertips will make his business more profitable and money means more to Elias than anything else.

6

Reunited

In the summer of 1950 Nadeem, Leila and their daughters finally arrive in the country following several long months at sea. Elias and Charbel wait anxiously at the Port of Sydney while their family clear customs before disembarking from the ship. Dressed sharply in tailor made suits purchased just for the occasion, the brothers beam with pride eager to show their family how well they have done since leaving Lebanon years ago. Unfortunately, they overlook just how uncomfortable it can get wearing suits during the hot summer months. Their bodies sweat profusely and now they need to keep their suit jackets on to conceal their soaking wet shirts, and so they are hotter than ever. Alas they think it's worth it, dressed smartly like this will show off their success, proof that the years apart have been worth it. With their eyes fixed on the arrival gate they can hardly wait to be united with their family. Once the brothers see their mother, they leap with joy and run towards her, Leila hugs her sons tightly, kissing them as a gush of happy tears stream down her face.

'Finally, we are all together, my sons how I have missed you.' She cries out loudly in Arabic.

The Anglo-Australian passengers watch Leila's outpouring of affection in disgust. Stoic and unemotional they find her behaviour very strange and unacceptable and Leila instantly senses that she is not welcome in her new homeland. Even so, for now she ignores their cruel judgement, happily distracted by this moment of overwhelming joy, Leila holds her sons tightly. Nadeem shows much less emotion than his wife, despite all these years of separation, he hugs each of them with little affection. While Elias has his back turned, Nadeem kisses Charbel smiling at him and Leila watches disapprovingly, she hoped Nadeem might change but sadly it does not seem so. The brothers hug their sisters lovingly surprised at how much they have grown, the girls are woman now, sadly for them this means Nadeem will arrange their marriages as soon as possible.

The entire family move straight into their new house, a kind gift from Elias and Charbel. Whilst Leila and her daughters revel in delight at having a new home, Nadeem takes the generous offering as an insult. Their home in Lebanon was gifted to him by his parents, and now he must accept his sons have done the same, his ego takes a blow. He pledges to himself that come hell over high water his position as provider for this family will be restored. For now, he must accept the way things are and hope that his community are too distracted in their own lives to notice, some are already settled in Sydney and the rest are barrelling across the sea in droves soon to arrive in Australia. And so, from this day forward Nadeem begins to plot how to restore the balance of power so he may once again hold firmly the status of family patriarch. Worst still, he resents that Elias has helped provide their new home, the son of a poor family, the stepson that has no tie to Nadeem's bloodline. Meanwhile the brothers are oblivious to Nadeem's spiteful jealousy, with an intent only to make certain their family settle comfortably in a land so foreign and far away from their Lebanon.

Although the house is new, it is very small with three tiny bedrooms, a combined kitchen and lounge room, and a bathroom with a shower and no bathtub, the toilet is located outside in the backyard. The sisters share one of the bedrooms, as do the brothers and Nadeem and Leila take the third bedroom. Their backyard is large by local standards, but pales in comparison to the one back home which boasted endless stretches of green mountainous countryside. Adjusting to this new country will be a challenge for the family but Leila does not complain, she is very proud of her sons and having the family together again is all that she can ask for. Nadeem on the other hand, quickly takes aim at his sons, complaining that the house is far too small.

For many years now the brothers have had to grudgingly tolerate Australian food, annoyingly that Lebanese restaurant nearby their flat never did open. Leila's heart sank every time she received a letter from her sons complaining about the food, and about how much they missed her delicious meals. So now she sets about making sure those days are behind them. Accordingly on the very first day of their arrival she promptly sends her sons off to the markets to gather all the ingredients she needs to prepare a feast of home cooked Lebanese dishes. When she hands Elias the list of ingredients he stares sadly at her, she has no idea.

'We can't get any of that.' He explains in Arabic. 'We have tried for years.'

'Take me to the store with you.' Leila insists, balking at the suggestion she won't be able to cook their traditional meals.

And so, Leila goes to the grocery store with her sons, thrilled to be riding in a car, she can't believe her sons own a car. When they finally arrive at the store nearby their old neighbourhood Leila can't believe her eyes, there is barely enough stock to cook a basic Lebanese meal let alone the feast she had in mind. She is heartbroken but has her own ideas about how she will fix this problem.

'I know what to do, we need to visit some people.' She insists. 'There are families from our village who surely must know where to get proper ingredients.'

Several other families from their village have already settled into the country so Nadeem and Leila want the boys to drive them around to each house so they can visit and hopefully come away with some groceries, or at least have better ideas on where to get them. Elias holds his head down when his father suggest they take Charbel's Chevrolet rather than Elias' less than impressive ute. The Chevrolet was a pricy but proud purchase for Charbel and predictably Elias skimped on what he was willing to pay for a vehicle. Normally Elias would defend his purchase as smart, having saved money by buying a cheap economical car, but watching Nadeem smile proudly at Charbel distracts him. It's as though all the confidence he built up over the past four years just fades away in an instant. With Nadeem around again, the feeling of dread quickly creeps back into his life.

Their daughters are not allowed to come along for the ride as they must tend to domestic chores, but more to the point, Nadeem does not want them out in public. He fears his girls might be led astray and does not want them exposed to young Australians that behave and think sinfully, he has heard enough stories to be concerned. His daughters must be kept virtuous for any family to consider them as potential brides for their sons.

On their visits Leila manages to gather some seedlings and plants from her old neighbourhood friends, fortunately her neighbours had the foresight to pack a variety of plant and herb seeds in their luggage when they left the old country. Leila is excited because now she can plant a garden of vegetables in her backyard. While she bargains with her old neighbour over what she can and cannot take from their garden, Nadeem stays inside to discuss matters in preparation for Nayla's betrothal. He will worry about the other children later, but for now Nayla is getting old.

Three months pass, and the family has settled into their new home and thankfully the sweltering summer heat begins to ease as cooler autumn temperatures bring much needed relief. The welcome cool change means a drop in the number of hot sleepless nights the family has endured over summer. Apart from Elias and Charbel the family has never experienced a summer like this, back in the village the cool mountain breeze always kept their home cool at night making it possible to sleep. Charbel wants Elias to help pay for an air-conditioning system so the family can sleep better at night. Elias hates seeing his family suffer through the harsh Australian summer months, but the cost of running the unit is extremely high and that is harder for him to accept. In the end he suggests they purchase an industrial size fan for the living room, and they can sleep on the floor when it gets too hot. Although his heart is in the right place, Elias struggles to part with money. Even so, he tries hard to help his family cope with the heat by encouraging them to sit on the veranda late at night awaiting the cool southerly change. He also hoses down the roof and outside walls later in the day to take the sting out of the heat, but it never works. Cold showers at night and sitting outside on the veranda is the way they manage.

The summer months also prove challenging for Leila and her vegetable garden which now takes up most of the backyard. Lebanese cucumbers line the fence, tomato plants pop up in patches all over, and the vast number of corn stalks are so tall their backyard looks like a jungle. She takes extra care with her herb garden of endive, parsley, mint, oregano, and thyme, without these plants she couldn't cook for her family. Leila has done everything possible to protect her plants from the burning sun and doesn't care what her neighbours think about the lengths she will go to achieve this. Some of her methods are quite strange and the neighbours complain to council often. She has erected a makeshift tarpaulin from bed sheets to create shade to protect the young fruit trees and vegetable garden. The neighbours stare over the fence disapprovingly but it does the job and Leila just ignores her new enemies. She waters her plants day and night, pulls out weeds and plows the soil with pick and shovel like a machine, and thankfully it all pays off.

Leila's meticulous efforts and steely determination means her family will soon enjoy the kind of fruit and vegetables they grew up eating, she will be able to cook Lebanese dishes for them using the right herbs and vegetables. She needs her family to feel at home in this far away land because going back to Lebanon is not an option, it would mean living a life of poverty for all of them. Although Leila fought hard to stop Elias from leaving Lebanon, she now understands, he had the foresight to see that Australia was their opportunity to escape poverty, to avoid what they both had endured so many years ago.

Her efforts to provide for the family has resulted in the creation of a tiny farm, and a makeshift fire-pit to cook fresh Lebanese bread. The neighbours complain to the police claiming this outlandish contraption will burn the whole neighbourhood down, but the police come by without laying charges, happy to accept fresh loaves of Lebanese bread cooked in that very fire-pit, a harmless bribe they think.

The one thing Leila struggles to find is burghul, cracked wheat as the Australians refer to it. She needs this ingredient to make her tabouli, the traditional Lebanese salad of parsley, tomato, onion, burghul drenched in olive oil and lemon juice, a dish her family sorely miss. There is no way of sourcing burghul from anywhere, so she decides to make her own. Leila orders Elias to go out and buy bulk whole wheat groats so she can lay them out flat in the backyard. This way the whole wheat can dry out in the sun until they crack. Leila plans to grind the cracked wheat with her stone grinder they brought with them on the boat on route to Australia. Once word gets around that she is producing her own bulgur, their village friends will come begging for it and Leila plans to sell it, or barter for other ingredients she needs.

Leila has one more venture up her sleeve, but it will be a tricky one because she knows the neighbours will call the police and she can only spare so much food to bribe them with. She wants to grow her own grapes and then ferment them and finally process through a distill, this way Nadeem will be able to enjoy the traditional Lebanese hard liquor, arak once again. She deliberates and finally decides to hold off for now because her sons have begged her to, there are far too many complaints being made about the family now, they are not very popular in their neighbourhood.

Unsurprising the family stand out as odd in this predominantly Anglo-Australian neighbourhood, but Leila just ignores them and goes about her business, she can't communicate in their language so makes no effort to try and explain her ingenious endeavours. Elias begs his mother to hold off from buying live chickens and a lamb, just for a few more months while the dust settles.

Nadeem has been helping Leila with her activities but feels increasingly redundant around the house and wants to go out to work. With Leila attracting a lot of attention from the neighbours and Nadeem going stir crazy without work, Elias decides it's time to get his parents to help in the shop. Although Elias' sisters could help, Nadeem forbids it. He does not want his daughters outside their home, exposed to a culture he considers immoral, he must keep them pure prior to marriage. And so, the girls are directed to stay home and oversee the garden, keep the home clean and cook the evening meal.

Leila finds she has way too much time on her hands since being forced to stay out of the garden and is deeply resentful at her nosey neighbours for it. Although she will be busy helping in the shop very soon, it doesn't help her now, accordingly Leila decides to get more involved with the church.

So far, finding a suitable place of worship has proven most difficult and this is despite her son's efforts to help her look for one. They have driven their mother to many suburbs around where they live to find something to her liking. They are losing their patience because this errand has swallowed up much of their free time, which isn't much at all. Leila refuses to go to a church without an Arabic speaking priest, so that rules out every church within a 15-kilometre radius of their house. She also dislikes the fact that every church they have come across so far does not have a statue of Saint Charbel, the patron Saint of Lebanon. She misses the chanting and singing during mass and the smell of incense that fills the church like a cloud of smoke from heaven. They live in a neighbourhood so foreign to their village back home and the brothers are frustrated their mother can't accept that.

After a month of searching in their area Elias gives up and decides the only way his mother will be happy is if they go to his old church in Redfern, it's traditional Maronite and that will suit her. The travel time is challenging but it's worth it seeing his mother so happy. Nayla is also delighted by this; she remains deeply devoted in her unwavering faith. Mass continues to be an important part of the family's life and it's pleasing that they can now understand their priest. The brothers can only drive their family to church on Sundays due to their work. Leila and her daughters continue to attend the local church on the other days, despite not being able to understand the English-speaking priest, they pray in Arabic throughout the mass instead. The parishioners watch in amazement wondering if they are speaking in tongues. Nadeem uses this time to visit members of his community, aiming to plant the seed and pave the way for the betrothal of his children. The brothers work long hours so are excused from attending church daily, but they are expected to go to mass every Sunday without fail.

Nayla loves going to church, in fact her devotion to God and mission to become a nun has grown stronger. She is extremely devout and prays every waking moment of the day. This annoys her sisters because when she throws herself into deep prayer, they end up having to do all the chores around the house without her help. They cunningly tease her threatening that she'll go to hell for her laziness and unwillingness to help them, from that moment forward Nayla does all her chores and prays as she does them. Her sisters watch and laugh as she chants and dusts at the same time, but Nayla doesn't care, she won't risk missing out on going to heaven for anything.

Although Nadeem claims to be a religious man he loathes Nayla's devotion to God, he boils with rage when she chants and prays believing this will discourage her from wanting to marry. Rather than respecting his daughter's deep devotion to her faith and supporting the vocation she dreams of, he thinks it's ridiculous and is infuriated by it. He believes God wants for his daughters to enter a good marriage and have lots of children, this is the role of a woman. Why would God object to that he tells his wife in fury. Leila knows her husband's real motive and that it has nothing to do with being a religious man. She knows that what he really cares about is his reputation, any hint of tarnishing the family name concerns him, if he can't marry his daughter off that reflects poorly on him and his family name. Sadly, Leila is too afraid to challenge his views, and so Nayla has little hope of getting what she wants. Although Nayla is a beautiful woman, she is getting on in her years and he thinks she might be too old to attract a good prospective Lebanese husband with her childbearing years quickly fading away. Accordingly, he continues to work hard to find her a husband and has made it clear that she will never become a nun and will marry the man he chooses for her. Nayla prays desperately each day, pleading with God to stop her father, to convince him that she should instead devote her life to the church, as a nun.

So far all of Nadeem's attempts to arrange meetings between Nayla and a prospective husband have been met with resistance. She always has an excuse for not being able to show up to the meeting, like a headache or stomach-ache. Lately though, Nadeem has threatened her with violence and often beats her for defying him. Terrified for her daughter, Leila tries to convince Nayla that Nadeem will never back down, and that she should just try and be open to the possibility of a marriage, telling her perhaps that's what God wants for her.

'How do you know this one won't be a good husband?' Leila begs Nayla to consider.

'I won't marry anyone mother, my calling is to be a nun.' She cries begging her mother to understand.

'Why do you think you have a choice my poor daughter?' Leila sobs. 'I'm terrified he'll hurt you my sweetheart, please don't be so stubborn.'

'I have to do what God has chosen for me, my life is to serve God, not to be a wife.' She insists.

The violence and intimidation continue with the terrible beatings from her father becoming so frequent that Nayla begins to fear for her life, sadly she eventually backs down and accepts her fate giving in to her father's demands. Perceived as old for marriage, her options are very limited, accordingly the only prospective husband Nadeem can find is Anton, Nayla's second cousin. Intermarriage, customary in Lebanon at the time is something Nadeem has no issue with. An extremely traditional man, he will never assimilate into what he considers an impure Australian way of life. Like Nadeem, Anton is a cruel and unkind man and because no one else will marry Nayla her fate is sealed, she will be forced to marry a beast, just like her mother did. Charbel hates what Nadeem is doing to Nayla, he wants his sister to be happy, not married off to an awful man. He knows how devoted she is to God and understands why she wants to become a nun, but he is too afraid to say anything, nobody in the family is brave enough to stand up to Nadeem. This awful predicament sends him into a panic as he wonders what would happen if his father found out about Hilda. He has turned down so many offers of marriage and his father is growing suspicious.

Unlike Charbel, Elias shares his stepfather's dogmatic views, he believes Nayla should marry and forgo this idea of becoming a nun. In his opinion she'll regret the decision not to marry later in life, realising only when it is too late, missing out an opportunity to enjoy the blessings of her own family. Even so, Elias is unhappy about the man Nadeem has chosen for Nayla, but also understands there are no other choices. He hates that Nadeem beats up his poor sister, but like everyone else, he won't say anything, Nayla is on her own.

Tonight, Nayla lays restlessly in her bed unable to sleep, filled with dread and sick with worry, she is unable to drown out the awful thoughts of what will become of her life now that she will be forced to marry. For weeks she hasn't been able to think about anything else other than this impending betrothal that will deny her calling from God, now she will never become a nun. Since childhood she has known her vocation, to devote herself to God. But now she is being forced to deny her calling, how can she do that, the thought haunts her. At least her sisters will be spared from what she is about to face, a life of sadness with a terrible man. Nadeem will worry about his younger daughters next; he must settle his oldest daughter's marriage first. And so, for now her sisters lay peacefully submerged in a deep slumber as they enjoy happy dreams, not the nightmare she is living out.

Hours pass and Nayla still can't sleep, her pillow is soaked with tears, she can barely compose herself. This was forced onto her; the beatings became unbearable and now she will be denied her calling. She has been praying all night, begging God to change her father's mind, to soften his heart but the prayers go unanswered, as they have done for months. She wonders if perhaps she has been praying for the wrong thing, with a heart as cold as ice her father will surely never change, no miracle in the world could temper the ego that drives his motives.

Praying to soften his heart is impossible because Nadeem has ignored God's will, and suddenly she understands what to do, and it terrifies her, she must leave her beloved family. Crippled with fear she understands the sacrifice, her Cross to bear in life will be to lose all her family, because there will be no turning back once she leaves. And so now she prays for strength, protection, and insight into how exactly she will do this, wondering how on earth to plot her escape, she decides that through blind faith she will find a way.

Filled with panic and dread Nayla quietly creeps out of bed and impulsively packs her clothes in the dark as her sister's sleep. She is ill prepared and unable to think clearly, not sure what clothes to pack. She can barely see in the dark corner of her room with only thin rays of moonlight poking through the blinds. Fearful she'll awaken her sisters; Nayla decides only to take a few items of clothing and quietly packs them into a plastic bag her mother left in the room for dirty laundry. With all her belongings in one plastic bag she quietly hurries out of the room, wiping away silent tears as she wonders if she will ever see her darling sisters again. She desperately wants to kiss and hug them goodbye, but she can't, that would wake them, and they will surely try to stop her. Her heart ponds as she passes her parent's room, wiping tears from her cheeks and then slips by her brother's room barely able to keep her composure.

She finally escapes out the front door with nothing more than the clothes on her back and a few belongings in a plastic bag. Nayla has no idea where to go, but she knows she can't stay here. She has not thought through her escape, it was a panicked act of desperation that drove her to this point, she has no idea where she will go and how to get there. Suddenly Nayla wishes this was just a bad dream, that she was safely tucked away in her bed fast asleep dreaming there with no impending marriage waiting to steal away her purpose in life. Only now it is too late, she has left the house in the dead of night, who knows what her father will do when he finds out, at the very least he will beat her senselessly whilst her mother watches in horror unable to protect her.

At a point of no return Nayla hurries onto the street in the darkness of night, barely able to see ahead of herself with the pathway poorly lit by dim council lights. Her heart pounds as she edges away from her home trembling with fear, but then she stops dead in her tracks. The reality of this flawed escape hits hard like a tonne of bricks, and she bursts into tears. She hurries back to her home and sits on the lawn at the foot of a tree that stands tall in front of her house. Her father will find her in the morning, and she will have to endure a dangerous flogging as well as her inevitable marriage to Anton, but for now she sits in shock under the tree too terrified to go back into the house.

From nowhere a car appears at the top of the street with headlights turned off, the vehicle slowly cruises towards Nayla's house. Paralysed with fear she can't move even though her instincts tell her to run. As if things couldn't get worse, she notices that it is Charbel's car, this terrifies her but at the same time it's baffling. What is he doing out this late at night she grapples to understand. Charbel notices Nayla sitting in the front yard in the dead of night and is horrified by this. Suddenly from nowhere, Nayla finds the courage to spring to her feet and darts off down the street, prompting Charbel to leap out of his car to chase after her. He catches up easy enough and grabs Nayla by the arm to stop her from getting away. She stares at him panicked by what he'll do to her, but Charbel looks just as scared, clearly both think they have been caught out.

'What are doing out here in the dark?' Charbel demands to know as he whispers loudly at her in Arabic.

Nayla's face is covered in tears, but she doesn't answer overwhelmed by her shame. Her face is badly bruised, and her cracked lip caked in dry blood, no doubt from another beating tonight. She begins to panic as her eyes swell with tears, she breakdowns sobbing uncontrollably.

'I don't know what I am doing, and I don't know where to go. Please don't tell father, I can't stand the beatings anymore.' She stops to compose herself wiping tears from her face.

'I can't marry him, my calling is to serve God, but father doesn't understand. I don't know what to do.' She sobs.

Charbel stares sadly at his sister, heartbroken by what his father has done to her.

'I have lost all will to live, I don't know what to do.' She stares at him in deep despair.

'I will help you.' He promises her.

'How can you help?' She wonders in confusion.

'I have a friend that you can stay with, she is kind and will not hurt you. Please trust me I would never leave you in danger.' He promises her.

'Perhaps God has answered my prayers.' Nayla stares at him with hope.

'You can't change your mind now, when we leave there is no turning back, you understand?' Nayla nods nervously, trusting her brother with her life.

It's well past midnight when Charbel and Nayla walk inside a building of units, finally able escape the bitter cold. Nayla nervously trails behind her brother as they ascend two flights of stairs. Once they reach the second floor Charbel heads toward the front door of an apartment and knocks gently, careful not to wake the neighbours. Nayla trembles with fear as she waits with her brother for someone to answer. Fatigued and sleep deprived, she can barely stand, still wishing this was just one big bad dream. Suddenly the door opens, and Hilda looks surprised to see Charbel, and shocked by the sight of the beautiful young stranger standing next to him, their visit snaps her out of a sleepy daze.

'This is my sister Nayla.' Charbel says in English, providing a quick explanation to his jealous beloved. 'Can we please come inside; I will explain everything.' He begs quietly careful not to awaken anyone. Nayla is confused by her brother's conversation, sadly the girls never learnt English, another form of control at the hands of their father.

No longer seeing any threat to losing her man, Hilda invites them both into her apartment and closes the door. As the door shuts Nayla bursts into tears, she clutches her brother's arm terrified by the reality of her situation. Here she stands in the middle of the night in this stranger's apartment, what will become of her once her father finds out, she wonders in terror. Filled with fear and dread she knows her father will never accept her back into the family home now. Her actions will bring shame and humiliation to the entire family for generations to come and she can't help but blame herself. A good daughter would be at home asleep in bed, getting all the rest needed in preparation for the big day, her impending marriage. What on earth has she done she wonders; she shudders to think about the consequences for her actions. She feels numb with fear as all these questions come to mind.

Charbel knows his sister is terrified, he holds her tightly trying to comfort her and Hilda watches in pity at the poor soul. She knows about their home life, Charbel has told her everything.

'Hilda is a good kind woman, and she will help you, please trust me, Nayla.' Charbel tries to reassure her speaking in Arabic.

'I must speak to her in Arabic.' Charbel explains to Hilda. 'It's the only language she understands, Nayla doesn't even speak French.'

Hilda smiles at Nayla which puts her at ease somewhat and she does sense genuine warmth from this stranger, but Nayla is terrified of her despite all her brothers' words of reassurance. Nayla has not mixed with anybody outside of her family and community so this is overwhelming, there is little Hilda can do to calm her.

'Can my sister stay with you for a while, she has been beaten every day since first resisting her betrothal, if she goes home now, she'll be forced to marry, or worse, who knows what my father will do. I will gladly pay for her share of the rent.'

'Keep your money, of course she can stay.' Hilda smiles at Nayla.

Charbel kisses Hilda and Nayla looks shocked by the sign of affection, they're not married so she can't understand what is happening.

'Hilda is my girlfriend.' He explains nervously to Nayla in Arabic. 'She says it's ok for you to stay.'

Nayla stares at Charbel in disbelief, shocked that she is not the only one that has defied their father wishes. She smiles nervously at Charbel, comforted a little by the fact that she is not the only one that has potentially cast shame onto their family name.

'Thank you, thank you.' She offers her gratitude to Hilda in Arabic.

'She is grateful and thanks you.' Charbel explains.

'Tell Nayla she is safe with me, and no one will know where she is. I will help her find a job and she will be ok.'

Charbel explains this to her and suddenly Nayla looks unsettled.

'No, I don't want to work, I want to be a nun, it is my calling. I have not left my entire family for no reason.' She insists.

'Ok Nayla, calm down if this is what you truly believe, then I will help you.' He holds her hand reassuringly.

Nayla smiles nervously, struggling to fathom her new reality, but God will give her courage, He will guide her, she tells herself.

'You better go, before they wake and find out that you are not home and that Nayla is gone, there will trouble otherwise, please hurry.' Hilda begs her love.

Charbel kisses Hilda and then hugs his sister tightly, trying to re-assure her she will be safe. 'I will come again later tomorrow.' He tells Nayla. She smiles nervously as he heads out the door.

Charbel manages to slip back into the house without waking anyone, he has done it many times before to see his love, sneaking out as soon as the family retire for the evening and quietly crawling back through the window late at night. Even so, tonight is very different, and he feels sick with worry wondering if he has just made a terrible mistake. What is done is done he tries to convince himself and he can't undo that. He quietly enters his bedroom and climbs into bed; he keeps his clothes on careful not to make any noise that may awaken his brother. Once his head touches the pillow he feels a great sense of relief, grateful that Elias knows nothing about what has just happened. Charbel couldn't possibly deal with any confrontation from his brother tonight, he needs a few hours of sleep to clear his mind so he can deal with the trouble that the morning will bring. When his parents discover Nayla has gone, he knows there will be turmoil, his poor mother will fall apart wondering where her precious daughter has gone, and his father will be filled with a dangerous rage. Charbel feels sick with worry thinking about it and tries to calm himself down, but suddenly things spiral out of control, to his horror Elias sits up in bed, Charbel trembles in fear as he discovers his brother has been awake this whole time.

'Where have you been?' Elias demands angrily. 'To see Hilda?' He asks seething with rage.

All blood drains from Charbel's face, he is terrified and goes numb with shock.

'Of course, you have.' Elias snaps.

'You know that, so why ask?' He insists nervously. 'I can't bear to be apart from her anymore, I'm in love.'

'It's deceitful, don't you have a conscience?' Elias taunts.

'It's not fair, why shouldn't I marry the woman I love?'

'She is not one of us fool. Don't you care about what others will think and say about our family? No one from our community will want to marry anyone of us if they find out about your disgraceful behaviour.'

'I can't stand to live without her.'

'Can you hear yourself?' Elias stares at his brother in shock. 'Don't you care about how this effects the rest of us? Wait until he finds out.'

'He expects too much and at our cost, look at what he has done to Nayla. The cruelty is unbearable to watch.'

'If Nayla was less rebellious and stubborn, she would see that he only wants the best for her.'

'Can you hear yourself? Anton is a terrible man. He beats his own mother. Why would he allow this betrothal knowing that?'

'She is getting old; this is the best chance of marriage she'll have. Do you want her to be a lonely old spinster?' Elias insists.

'I can't understand you; she wants to devote her life to God; we should praise her for that.'

'Just wait and see how happy Nayla will be, she will not regret it once she has her children.' Elias promises.

There is a moment of silence as Charbel struggles to decide whether to tell Elias the truth or just wait until the morning when everybody else finds out. He can't wait, he must tell.

'She won't marry, she left her home tonight.' Charbel trembles as he speaks.

'What?' Elias yells. This startles both realising it could stir the household out of a deep sleep. Both brothers sit in silence waiting to see if anybody stirs, and after a few minutes they breathe easy thankful the family continues to sleep.

'I took her to Hilda's place; I saw her running down the street tonight in a terrible state and I had to take her somewhere safe. I couldn't sit back and allow her to marry that monster and deny her calling from God.'

'Are you crazy? Do you know what you have done?' Elias seethes as he whispers.

'I know what I have done, I know it will cause a lot of trouble, but I couldn't let this happen to her, she was desperately sad.'

'You fool, he'll find out about you and Hilda.'

'I don't care, I'm sick of lying and I won't let them wonder where their daughter has gone, they need to at least know she is safe.'

'Don't be stupid, they will disown you. I will lose both a brother and sister overnight.'

'I don't know what else to do?' Charbel crumbles in anguish.

'I will write a note to them pretending it's from Nayla. They will think she has left home to join a church far from here, to become a nun one day. I will lie to our parents for you.' He snaps at his brother bitterly.

'They'll worry about her; I want them to know she is safe.'

'Are you stupid? Our reputation is at stake here, if we say she has run away to the church the community will pardon her actions as madness. If we tell the truth they'll call our sister a whore, our honourable reputation will go down the toilet just like that.'

'They'll know it's not her writing, she writes like a twelve-year-old.' Charbel insists.

'Then I'll write like a twelve-year-old.' Elias insists, annoyed by all the trouble his brother has caused.

'I only did this because I love Nayla.' Charbel tries to make his brother understand.

'Enough, go to sleep, I'll write the letter now before they wake. There will be trouble in the morning, and we will need all our strength.'

Months pass on from that awful morning which played out exactly how Elias predicted, Nayla is now disowned from her family. That is not true for Leila who secretly hopes her daughter will return to her one day, although she must hide her anguish. Nadeem will never forgive Nayla for the damage she has done to the reputation of his family, the entire village community have judged her actions as disgraceful, how could she as an unmarried woman leave her family and home. Regardless of her good intentions, the act is unforgivable. Nadeem will never allow her back into their home and now must mop up the mess and pay the price for her unpardonable actions, there could be no greater blow to his ego.

Leila has wept daily in private since the day her daughter left, Nadeem's decision to disown their daughter has broken her. Her children are her life, to be separated from any of them causes her unbearably pain. She wonders how anybody could judge Nayla's actions as shameful, her daughter gave up her life to serve God. Even so, she keeps her thoughts to herself as it would be dangerous to share this truth with her husband. Filled with deep sorrow Leila misses her daughter terribly, but she could never set out to find Nayla, who knows what Nadeem would do to her.

To distract from Nayla's actions and the damage it has caused to the family's reputation, Nadeem throws a big wedding to celebrate his next daughter's marriage to Anton. Accordingly, tonight the community celebrates the marriage of Zahra to Anton, an awful man that will make his new wife's life miserable. Nadeem knows in his heart that Anton is a bad choice but nobody else from the community will allow their son to marry into Nadeem's family, not now while the outrageous actions of Nayla are fresh in their minds.

Zahra has no say of course, she knows she can't object, her father has made it frightfully clear what will happen if she does not obey him. She is terrified of following in her sisters' footsteps, where would she go? She doesn't even speak English, nor does she know anyone outside of her family and community. Worst of all, she would never see her family again, she would be banished just like Nayla, and so Zahra reluctantly goes ahead with the marriage. She must put on a performance in front of the crowd of guests celebrating the marriage between herself and Anton. An entire month of tears has left Zahra with no fight and so she will marry a man she does not love, a man that fills her with fear and dread, this will be her new life.

Charbel watches on saddened by this awful union, he knows his sister will miss out on an opportunity to share her life with a man that loves her and raise children with a man who will be kind to them. Although Elias understands why Nadeem has arranged this betrothal, he loathes the idea that it is Anton that she must marry, and so he fears for his sister's future. Of course, nobody will say anything and so Zahra's future of unhappiness begins today, on her wedding night.

Later in the evening the formalities of the wedding end and most of the older guests begin to leave, the rest of the crowd stay on to enjoy their evening of chatter, drink, and dance. Nadeem and his sons sit quietly at a table drinking arak. Mary, an attractive young woman sits at their table next to her father. Elias has not been able to keep his eyes off Mary the entire evening, he remembers her well from the village, there were many times she came to the general store with her mother, and even back then he was spellbound by her beauty. Mary has also been staring at Elias throughout the evening, although as discreetly as possible, there is mutual attraction no doubt. Nadeem pays a lot of attention to Mary because she comes from a good family, a family that has been extremely successful since migrating to Australia. She would make the perfect wife for Charbel and the obvious attraction between her and Elias annoys him.

The entrancement between the two is suddenly interrupted by loud music that begins to blare as a swarm of young adults, mainly women descend upon the dance floor to dance the dabke, a traditional Middle Eastern dance. To dance the dabke the young folk interlock their arms, tap, and stomp their feet, and sing and chant loudly. Mary gets a nudge from her father to get up and join in. Charbel wants to dance, but Elias doesn't as he is much more reserved than his brother. Simon, Mary's father smiles at the boys.

'Why don't you both go up there to dance, your father and I have matters to discuss.' He insists, speaking in Arabic.

The brothers shake their heads politely, suddenly aware that the discussion they are about to have will impact one of them.

'Ok, that's fine.' Simon smiles.

Elias sits anxiously hoping that Mary's father sees him as a good match for his daughter. Charbel looks nervous, dreading any suggestion that he might be a good match for Mary. Simon watches the brothers in amusement, knowing he holds all the cards to this decision. Seeing the angst in their faces, he decides he's had enough fun and puts an end to the anxious wait.

'I think it is clear who Mary should marry.' Simon informs Nadeem as he looks over at Elias.

'Yes, Charbel will be perfect for Mary.' Nadeem insists and Elias stares at his stepfather in fury.

'I meant your other son; Elias would be a good match for my daughter.' Simon insists.

'Well, we have different views, so maybe we should discuss this again another time when we have thought more about it.' Nadeem insists pompously.

Mary's father is not impressed but nods to keep the peace. Enraged, Elias gets up to leave, but addresses Simon politely before leaving.

'Thank you, sir, Mary is a wonderful girl, I like her very much.' Elias hopes this will turn the tables in his favour. He heads outside to cool off and Charbel follows, leaving Nadeem and Simon to sit in awkward silence.

When the family return home later that evening it is without Zahra, she must now go and live with Anton's family because the newlyweds don't have a home of their own. Anton has no savings, he has never been able to keep a job on account of his dreadful temper, he gets fired after only a couple of weeks of starting a new job. Accordingly, he has no money to go towards the purchase of a house for himself and his new bride. Anton's parents are at their wits end not sure what to do about him, and now the luckless Zahra must put up with this very sad situation and God help her when the children come.

Everyone except Nadeem feel the sombre absence of Zahra tonight, but there are more immediate troubles brewing in the household to distract them. Nadeem is heavily intoxicated by a full night of drinking, and he won't stop badgering Elias for getting in the way of his plans to have Charbel marry Mary. Elias has tried very hard not to retaliate knowing this will only make matters worse, it doesn't matter though because Nadeem is relentless in his attack.

'How dare you embarrass me like that, I am the head of this family, I make all the decisions, not you.' He shouts at Elias. 'You are an embarrassment to our family, what you did tonight was shameful.' Nadeem looks set to continue and suddenly Elias snaps, he can't take it anymore.

'Just tell the truth, this is not about respect, it's about getting what you want. You don't want me to marry Mary because she comes from a good family, they are wealthy and highly regarded amongst the community, so of course you prefer for your real son to marry into that. I've never been good enough for you, I grew up with that but no more. I want to marry Mary and I pray to God her father wants the same.'

'You are not good enough, it's true.' Nadeem stares abhorrently at Elias.

Leila and Charbel watch in anguish, too afraid to step in and stop Nadeem's cruel attack. Elias seethes desperate for Charbel to defend him, after all Elias has done for him, but Charbel does nothing which causes Elias to snap.

'How do you know if he even wants to marry Mary?' Charbel looks stunned that Elias would put him on the spot like that, and in such a terrible predicament. He stares nervously at his father but doesn't say anything.

Nadeem stares suspiciously at Charbel wondering why he hasn't responded.

Charbel trembles in fear, his father terrifies him so he can't tell the truth.

'No, I don't want to marry Mary, I love Elias, and I want him to be happy. He would make a good husband for Mary.' Charbel tries to back out of the trouble his brother has stirred.

'Shut up, you will marry Mary you fool.' Nadeem insists as he shouts at him. Charbel stares nervously at his father but then somehow manages to muster up the courage to speak his truth.

'No father, I don't want to marry Mary.' Charbel looks at Elias nervously, Elias shakes his head at his brother gesturing for him to shut up and say no more, but it's too late, Charbel can't hide his feelings for Hilda any longer. Elias regrets the trouble he has stirred; afraid he'll now lose his brother in the same way he lost Nayla.

'I'm in love with another woman'. He confides, so terrified he could throw up. 'She is not Lebanese, but I love her.' Charbel finally tells the truth, he can't imagine life without her.

Nadeem watches Charbel like a raging bull ready to pounce, Elias stares at his brother terrified for his safety, as does Leila, but before they can do anything Nadeem swiftly backhands Charbel hard across the mouth and the brutal attack leaves his face covered in blood. Leila screams at him to stop but he ignores her as he stares brutally at Charbel, disgusted by the revelation. Charbel takes the blow stoically and wipes blood from his face. Elias tries to pull Nadeem away from Charbel, but he smacks Elias hard across the face and pushes him into the wall. Leila stands in front of Nadeem to stop him from attacking her sons and before Nadeem can lay a hand on her the boys pull their mother away begging her to leave the room.

'Please leave him alone.' Leila begs Nadeem as she sobs. Nadeem stares venomously at Charbel.

'You will end it with this slut tonight or else leave this family and never come back.' He stares ruthlessly at his son as he delivers the ultimatum.

Charbel is raging inside but is too afraid of what harm Nadeem could do to his mother if he retaliates. A deathly silence fills the room.

'I will end it father.' Charbel lies as he retreats from the room having already made up his mind that he won't. He can't argue with this barbaric bull crazy enough to hurt his beloved mother, so Charbel tells him what he wants to hear to keep the peace for tonight. But he has made up his mind, he will have to walk away from the family he loves because he cannot stand a life without Hilda. Nadeem has forced him to choose between his beloved family and the love of his life, and it hurts terribly.

7

Going Separate Ways

Charbel and Nayla sit quietly inside a tiny church in Sydney's Inner West, so deep in thought they don't notice wedding guests have already beginning to arrive. Today Charbel will marry Hilda, and sadly Nayla will be the only member of his family attending the wedding, his father has made certain of it. Nadeem has not spoken to Charbel since he left that night some time ago. He has made no effort to try and contact his son since then and has forbidden his wife and children from making any contact with Charbel, which is heartbreaking for them. It has been three months since that night and Leila has cried every day since. Her only solace from her son's departure has been the revelation that Nayla was safely living with Hilda, Charbel could not stand to keep the truth from his poor mother. The separation from his brother has been devastating for Elias, they have never lived apart before. He deeply regrets what he did to Charbel, if only he never said anything that night, maybe his brother would still be with him now. He will have to live with the consequences of putting Charbel in a position where he had to come clean about Hilda, and inevitably make a choice over whether to leave her or not, Elias will have to live with the guilt for the rest of his days. Charbel sits soberly thinking about all of this on a day that should be filled with joy.

Most of the wedding guest are from Hilda and Charbel's workplace, no one from Hilda's will be attending. Sadly, most of her family perished during the Second World War and those who survived migrated to other parts of Europe, including her mother. Hilda's father died when she was very young and there were no other children after that, she remained an only child. Her mother never remarried and raised her daughter as a sole parent, an unusual practice at the time. Although raising Hilda all alone on a tiny income from working whenever Hilda was at school, her mother managed. She was a stoic woman, not distracted by the challenges of extreme poverty. She was resilient, resourceful, and strong willed and not only provided for her daughter's material needs, but also unknowingly became a strong role model to her. Hilda grew up to be just like her mother, so it was inevitable she would have no fear about courageously venturing halfway across the world alone to build a better life, sadly forcing mother and daughter apart by thousands of miles, and today Hilda regrets this for the first time. Neither bride nor groom will have their mother present on their very special day.

Charbel looks very handsome in a smart tuxedo that cost him a weeks' pay, even so he considers the money well spent because today he will marry the love of his life, his sweetheart Hilda. Nayla is dressed modestly already preparing for her eventual transition into the nunnery, she has already moved into the convent and is well on her way to becoming a nun. Nayla can see the joy in Charbel's eyes as he gets ready to marry his bride but doesn't miss the sadness looming over him that he tries to hide, she knows how devastated her brother is by the absence of family on this very important day. In their culture a wedding is a grand celebration that the entire family, immediate and extended not only attend but also get involved in, from planning to staging the big day. On top of that the entire village community are expected to join in to help the family celebrate, and today there is none of that.

'You look so sad on a day you should be happy.' Nayla stares empathetically at her brother.

'Yes, I know, but I don't want Hilda to see, this is her big day, and I don't want to spoil it. It's bittersweet, today I wed the love of my life but can't share that joy with all my family'.

'I know.' She looks sadly at her brother. 'But very soon you'll start a family of your own.' She smiles lovingly at him, hoping to cheer her brother up.

'Yes, you're right, I am very lucky in that way. But I have you too, I thank God I have you in my life little sister.' He smiles lovingly at Nayla. 'You will always be my family Nayla, even when Hilda and I have our own family. We will be one family, don't worry about that.'

'Thank you Charbel. You and Hilda have been very kind to me, and I love you both very much.'

Careful not to add further to her brother's anguish, Nayla keeps her deep thoughts to herself and ponders solemnly over what they have given up. She misses her family dreadfully, especially her mother. Not a day goes by when she is overcome with sorrow knowing she will never see them again. Although she has not said a word, Charbel can read her like a book.

'I know you are hurting; I miss them very much and think of our family every day. But this is a sacrifice we must make, there is no choice in it. We have lost most of our family and that is painful, but we can now live the life we have chosen. You will soon become a nun which makes me so proud, and I'll be with my beloved Hilda.' Charbel smiles lovingly at his sister, and she smiles.

'You are right, but I miss mother, it breaks my heart every day.

Charbel nods sadly, agreeing. So engrossed by their discussion neither has noticed how much time has passed, all the guests have poured into the church, and the music begins to play, at any moment the bride will appear at the entrance to the church. Nayla quickly gets up to take her seat but firsts hugs her brother lovingly and then hurries off to her seat.

As Hilda appears, Charbel springs to his feet to watch his bride begin to walk down the aisle, her manager standing proudly by her side, giving her away on a day her father cannot. Today Charbel starts a new life with his bride and is excited for everything that lays ahead for them, even if it means his beloved mother and siblings will not be a part of it.

Ten years on and Elias is married to Mary with a family of his own. When Charbel left, Nadeem had no logical reason to stand in the way of his stepson's desire to marry Mary. Any objection to the marriage would have drawn attention to his ulterior motive. Mary's father considered Elias a good match for his daughter, there was no reason to object with Charbel out of the picture. The deep resentment he had for Elias, a son spawn by another, was something he would need to keep to himself.

The first few years of their marriage are very happy ones, but sadly that doesn't last. With no uncertainty Elias loves Mary, she is a wonderful wife and model mother to their children. Even so, his obsession to build more and more wealth, to gain Nadeem's acceptance, serves to sabotage their marriage. His fixation on money distracts him from what is most important, the unconditional love of his wife and children. He takes for granted the deep love from both his immediate and extended families, and instead unknowingly focusses on gaining approval and love from his stepfather. Nothing will placate his obsession for acceptance from a man that will never love him, and overtime this ends up damaging a once happy marriage.

Over the past decade Elias has managed to build considerable wealth hoping it pleases Mary, but it does not. Mary comes from an affluent family and has never been taken by the trimmings that come with it. She saw something in Elias that was not tied to wealth, he was sensitive and kind when she knew him from the village. Much of what she liked about him years ago has all but disappeared.

Elias and his immediate family live in a nice home, one of the many that he has purchased over the last decade. Nadeem and Leila continue to live in the same house they moved into when they migrated to Australia. Zahra is still married to Anton who is every bit the beast she was forced to marry many years ago. They have five children and Anton cannot provide for them as he is unemployed most of the time, his parents washed their hands of him years ago. Out of pity for his sister and her children, Elias allows Zahra and her family to live in one of his houses, free of rent. This kind act gives Mary some hope Elias might change.

Zahra has every reason to leave Anton, but Nadeem forbids it, divorce is a shameful act, and he won't allow his family name to be dragged through the mud, not even for the sake of his daughter and grandchildren, his reputation means more to him. Samya was married off a long time ago and now lives with her husband and five children, thankfully her husband is much kinder than Anton and is a good provider. Nadeem and Leila always have a house full of grandchildren as

Zahra and Samya visit daily with their kids, Nadeem insists on seeing his grandchildren.

Elias and Mary have four children of their own, all under the age of nine. They have three girls, Leila, Claudia and Nada and a boy named Joseph, their youngest child. Elias is very strict with his children, they are not allowed to mix with Australian kids, that means all their friends must be Lebanese, preferably from his village. He is very suspicious of what children are being taught at school, in fact he happens to be distrustful of Australian people generally. The older he gets, the more small-minded, conservative, and traditional he becomes, eerily, Elias becomes more like his stepfather with each day. As it happens, Elias is not around very much to enforce his rules, he works very long hours at the shop, to build his growing wealth. Notwithstanding the children assimilate into the Australian culture and he doesn't even notice, Mary is far more lenient than her husband.

With Charbel long gone, Nadeem has treated Elias with a little more respect in recent time, showing tiny signs of approval, and moments of recognition for a job well done, mainly regarding Elias' profitable business and portfolio of investment properties. Elias unconsciously laps up whatever attention he can get, having craved it since childhood. The modest acts of kindness make Leila happy; she has watched her poor son hunger for Nadeem's affection for too many years. Although this makes Leila happy, she remains deeply distraught over the loss of her two children, Nayla and Charbel. Filled with dread since the day they left, Leila has begged Elias constantly to find Charbel and Nayla, even after ten years. Elias has made some effort to find his siblings, but the shop and his family have kept him busy. But he hasn't tried very hard, fearful that if he found his brother then father and son by blood may reunite, and perhaps things would go back to the way they were, Elias would be on the out yet once again.

Over the past ten years Elias has worked long hours in the shop, sometimes twelve to fourteen a day, and normally seven days a week. Mary has been left to raise the children on her own and the children barely see their father. Elias relies heavily on his parents to help in the shop because he does not want to pay for labour, he would rather keep the money in the family. Even so, he is distrustful of anyone outside the family, Zahra and Samya are busy raising their young children so he can't call on them for help. He spends most of his waking days in the shop and sees his parents far more than his immediate family. This drives an even bigger wedge between Elias and Mary's once happy marriage, they have grown apart.

One day Mary comes into the store with her children as she needs to gather groceries for the evening meal and does not have any money. Elias has become so obsessed with building his wealth that he controls all the money. This upsets Mary deeply, and it infuriates her parents who have grown quite critical of the way Elias treats their daughter.

Their daughters have not sat still since arriving in the shop, like most children their age they want to play. They race around the store playing tag and Nadeem watches his grandchildren disapprovingly. Unlike his sisters, Joseph clings to his mother's skirt nervously, perhaps picking up on Nadeem's fury. Even so, from an early age Joseph has stood out as a little different to his siblings, very timid and shy and not very talkative.

'You better take the children home; this is a place of business not a playground.' Nadeem snaps at Mary in Arabic.

Mary looks hurt but says nothing, she has become accustomed to Nadeem's lack of affection for her children, he certainly doesn't treat his other grandchildren like this. Mary has watched Zahra and Samya's kids run around in the shop many times, but Nadeem never objects. Leila stares sadly at her daughter-in-law and grandchildren knowing the truth, that Nadeem does not consider Elias and Mary's children like family, they are not of his blood. Her heart breaks watching history repeat itself, so she goes over to her grandchildren smiling lovingly at them, desperate to make them feel welcome.

'Take this.' Leila hands each child a bag of lollies. The girls leap with joy, while Joseph takes the treats cautiously from her. The children are clearly not spoilt, Elias rarely provides his children with anything other than necessities. He takes all the groceries that Mary has gathered and places the items into bags for her to carry.

'The children are not good for business; they will scare the customers away.' He pleads with Mary to understand. Staring angrily at her husband, Mary takes the bag from him and heads out of the shop with her young children in tow.

Later that evening Elias comes home after a long and tiring day in the shop, and he is tired. He walks into a hype of activity as the kids jump all over him hoping their father has brought them a surprise treat, they know the shop is full of lollies. This is the only time they get to see their father because Elias leaves for work at the crack of dawn when the kids are still fast asleep. He is tired and hungry but tries to muster some strength to show his kids the attention they crave, he understands too well what it feels like not to get that. He hugs and kisses each of his children and pulls a chocolate bar from his pocket for the kids to share. Mary frowns at the frugal gesture, annoyed because he has a shop full of chocolate and this is all he offers, but the kids don't care as they quickly devour the sweet taking two bites each. Mary is still cranky at Elias for the way she and the kids were treated at the shop today, she resents Nadeem's coldness towards their children and Elias' reluctance to stand up and defend his wife and children.

Finally, Elias sits down at the dinner table to eat his meal but frowns at the leftovers Mary has served him. She planned to serve him the same food she and the kids ate only an hour earlier, but he refuses to eat it, accordingly Mary must cook him a fresh meal. Of course, this means extra work for her, she has barely had a chance to sit down today. Mary has been with the children all day and has taken care of all the domestic chores on top of that, she too is exhausted but that doesn't seem to count as work in her husband's eyes. Elias makes the money for their family, and constantly reminds Mary of that, insisting what she does is not really work because it doesn't generate income.

When Elias finally does finish work at least he gets to relax, Mary on the other hand continues with her chores with no rest. After preparing something fresh for Elias to eat she must round up the kids and fight them into having a shower. This is tricky because the kids dodge her as she struggles to catch up with them, they decide it will be fun to play hide and seek with their poor mother. Mary is furious at them because she has no idea it's a game they are playing and considers their actions disrespectful. She is exhausted but Elias does nothing to help, he considers domestic duties to be her sole responsibility and believes he has worked hard enough. He has no real understanding of how hard his wife works, she takes care of four small children from dawn to dusk and carries out all domestic duties without any support.

Once Elias finally gets a chance to sit alone and eat his meal in silence, Claudia, his middle daughter appears from nowhere and hops onto a chair next to him. She looks sad and her eyes begin to fill with tears.

'Claudia, what's wrong?' He asks in Arabic.

'I hate school.' She confesses sadly, hoping not to upset her father who has already worked very hard today, she knows this because he overstates his plight constantly.

'Why? School will make you smart.' He tries to shift her thinking.

'They always call me a wog; they say I should go back to my own country. Isn't this my country?' She asks genuinely confused.

Suddenly he begins to boil with rage as he pushes his food aside.

'Mary.' He shouts. 'Mary come here now.' He yells again.

After a moment Mary appears in dripping wet clothing, the children pulled her into the shower with them and she is less than pleased. Elias shows no pity for poor Mary, he just wants to know how she handled those kids who taunted Claudia.

'What did the school do about those children that called Claudia a wog?' He interrogates her in Arabic.

Fed up with all the weight she must carry, Mary lets loose.

'The school never does anything, no matter how much I complain about it. But you never see it, you're always in that shop.' Mary retaliates, surprised by her outburst. Elias does not challenge; he knows she is right. Even so he is defensive.

'I work hard for this family, of course I'm at the shop a lot because that's how a business runs, so how do you expect me to have time to see what is going on at school?'

Mary has little patience for his excuses, he is at the shop all the time because he is obsessed with making more and more money, his kids should matter more to him is her view. To avoid a fight, she excuses herself.

'I have to go and check on the children, goodness knows what they are up to now.' Mary races out of the room to see what the kids have gotten up to now.

Claudia starts to cry because she hates it when her parents fight, and she doesn't know what to do about her problem at school, Elias feels bad for her.

'Look at me sweetheart.' He speaks kindly to Claudia.

'The next time they call you names I want you to tell them that your parents came to this country as immigrants, honest, free and without any criminal past. You tell them they descend from convicts, criminals. That will shut them up.'

Claudia smiles hesitantly at her father, not really understanding what he means by this. She hugs him and Elias smiles adoringly at his daughter. For some reason father and daughter have always had a special connection.

Seeing Claudia upset like that forces Elias to rethink the excessive hours he works in the shop, he needs to be around his children more so he can toughen them up, and he considers Mary's approach to parenting too soft. Accordingly, he decides that Sunday's will become a day of rest allowing him to spend more time with his family. He struggles with the thought of closing the shop on Sunday because this will mean less takings, a difficult pill for him to swallow. Even so he can't keep doing this, not being around to rub off on his kids means they'll never learn to stand up for themselves. He thinks Mary is too soft and is not teaching their children to fight back whenever they get bullied. Ironically, Elias never learned to stand up to Nadeem whenever he pushed him around.

On his first free Sunday after the family returns from Church, Elias gathers the kids together to share with them the tradition of making arak, a strong Lebanese alcoholic beverage. Mary rolls her eyes at this wondering what the neighbours will think, but she bites her tongue knowing that at least the children will finally get to spend some fun time with their father. To begin with Elias gets his children to help him carry large boxes of golden yellow grapes out of the garage. The grapes are getting old, that's the reason why he got them so cheap at the markets. Rather than throw them out and waste money Elias decides to make arak with the ageing fruit. The wooden crates holding the grapes are sealed shut with lids fastened tightly with thick metal stables. Elias uses his pocketknife to lift out the tightly fastened staples and his kids watch in fascination, they are not used to seeing their father do fun things. Once the boxes are open Elias pours all the grapes into an inflatable swimming pool that the kids received for Christmas last year, suddenly the children shriek in horror.

'No, that's for swimming.' Nada yells at her father to stop.

'Yes, I know but for now it's for squashing grapes with your bare feet.' He grins at her.

Suddenly intrigued the kids quickly flick off their shoes and jump up and down pleading to get this game started. Elias laughs as does Mary, too bad about the neighbours she thinks to herself, this is a rare moment of happiness for her family. Elias hops into the pool first and stomps onto the grapes with his bare feet showing the kids how it's done. He barely has a chance to demonstrate before the kids jump in after him and join in with their father as they all stomp over the grapes with their bare feet. The family laugh so hard it draws attention from a nosey neighbour who peers over the fence to see what this strange Lebanese family is up to this time.

After a fun filled half hour Elias steps out of the pool and the kids reluctantly follow. Mary hoses off everyone's feet and hands over some towels to her drenched family to dry off with, surprisingly she is enjoying herself. Once they are all dried up Elias heads back into the garage and his children follow attentively. He drags out a barrel from the garage with his children in tow and sets it close by the pool filled with squashed grapes. Handing each of his children a bowl, they are directed to scoop out the squashed grapes and pour that into the barrel. Another half hour later the barrel is full and Elias seals it with a lid, the kids watch in anticipation wondering what the next steps of this fun game will be.

'We wait a day and then you will all get a chance to stir the grapes.' Elias explains. 'We have to do this for three weeks while the grapes ferment.'

The kids look disappointed because they want to keep having fun and Elias knows it.

'Come with me.' He tells them and they follow their father back into the garage. Once back in the garage Elias pulls away a blanket unveiling a copper apparatus that he paid top dollar for. The still was a recent purchase from a family that arrived from Lebanon not long ago. Apart from Leila, the kids look puzzled wondering what this large copper tank is used for.

'We are going to make a very special Lebanese drink called arak that is only for grown-ups, not kids you must understand. In three weeks I will show you how it's done, it's a complicated process and I want you all to learn it so one day you will make it yourselves.'

'I think I know how it works father.' Leila surprises him. 'I heard grandfather talking about it, the grapes ferment and then it goes into this apparatus to be distilled into pure alcohol. Then you must do it a few times.'

Elias looks surprised and impressed by how smart his daughter is, granted he already knows she is very bright because she always tops her class at school. Unlike their extremely intelligent sister, the other kids still look puzzled.

'Come on, the pool is clean now.' Mary shouts out to the kids; she has already anticipated that it wouldn't be too long before boredom sets in. 'Go inside and put your swimming costumes on.'

The kids shriek with excitement and charge into the house to get dressed. Mary smiles at Elias and he smiles back, it feels a little bit like old times.

8

Australian or Lebanese

A month later the final stage of the distillation has concluded, and Elias has begun to carefully pour all his homemade arak into glass decanters, these were also purchased from the same family that sold him the still. He paid handsomely for the jars but only did it out of necessity, he knows that good arak must be stored well to preserve its quality. No one from their community has been able to get their hands on good quality arak, unlike back in the village where it's plentiful. Elias has seized the opportunity to make the potent spirit before anyone else, knowing well that it will be a profitable venture. He also sees this as a good way to make up for lost takings that he would normally make on a Sunday. Knowing there is high demand for good quality arak within the community, Elias makes sure to produce quite a lot of it. Not only will he profit handsomely from this investment, the community will praise him for it, sadly it's also another unconscious attempt to please his stepfather.

Overly consumed with making money and impressing his community, Elias overlooks including his children in this stage of the process, they are meant to be a part of this project. He had promised to show them how the process ends and has now missed another opportunity to spend time with his family. Although Elias truly wanted to spend time with his kids and expose them to aspects of his culture, he was too afraid of the risk they posed. Their tendency to get excited and eager to help meant endless possibilities of breakage. Disappointed, Mary wonders how she could have been so foolish to think that his children might, on this occasion, come before money.

Elias understands that in Australia homemade liquor is unlawful unless it's not sold, with this in mind he takes great care in choosing his buyers, a snitch would bring his entire venture to a quick death. If the police are tipped off, they will come to his house and dismantle the still and confiscate all his liquor. No doubt they will then indulge in it, these are the perks enjoyed by police at the time. Elias isn't planning to sell all the arak, he will gift some of it to his family, certainly Nadeem will expect a bottle or two. The arak will also make impressive gifts for celebrations such as weddings, baptisms and the like. Elias will also make sure he has a few bottles on hand for himself as he enjoys a glass or two of arak with his evening meal.

Sadly, his mini enterprise barely sees the light of day because a nosey neighbour quickly tips Elias off to the police. Two police officers come around to his house one Sunday afternoon and direct him to dismantle the distillery or face charges. Desperate to save his money spinner Elias attempts to bribe the officers with cartons of cigarettes that he keeps hidden in the ceiling of his house, they are stored safer there than in the shop. Without any hesitation from the officers Elias manages to seal a deal, the police are happy to turn a blind eye. Despite this, the mean-spirited neighbour stares over the fence directly at the police officers calling them out, and just like that the near successful bribe is sabotaged. The deal is dead, and the officers take down the still and confiscate the liquor, well at least they'll get to take the arak home. As it happens the neighbour wants blood insisting the liquor be poured down the sink and if not, he'll take it up with the local police station. The police are not happy, first they miss out of cigarettes and now the liquor.

In one afternoon, Elias loses his expensive still and priceless arak, he stares angrily at his nosey neighbour who continues to stare brazenly over the fence every so often. Mary stays inside with the children; she doesn't want them to witness any of this. She feels humiliated by all that has happened today but also annoyed at Elias for being so obsessed with money. He could have just kept the arak for relatives, instead he has embarrassed the entire family. They will be singled out again, this time not just because they look different, or have a strange garden or make a lot of noise, but now they are also unlawful in the eyes of their neighbours. Mary is also very angry at her neighbour because she knows his motivation to call the police comes from a place of deep hatred of foreign people, and she has little tolerance for racist people.

In the end this experience leaves Elias feeling extremely bitter at his neighbour and at Australian people in general. He struggles to understand why his neighbour took issue with something that did not affect or hurt him in any way, back home that would never have happened. There is a deep dislike of migrants by many in the Australian community and Elias and his family have felt it since first arriving in the country. They have been treated like outcast and Elias grows more bitter about this by the day, this incident has cemented in him a deep resentment towards Australians and their very different way of life.

Elias sleeps poorly that night, still seething from the loss of his precious still and good quality arak. All the time, effort, and money he put into making his arak has literally gone down the drain. The normal way things work is police confiscate the liquor and take it with them, pretending it will be tipped out, but anyone with an ounce of street sense knows the reality is they'll drink it. That wouldn't bother Elias so much because at least all his hard work would have count for something, but now nobody gets anything. Worst still, he loses the money it cost him to make the spirit and potential profit for sales, this eats away at him. He loathes his neighbour for pushing the police so hard, Elias knows that it is his neighbour's contempt for Lebanese people, a motive driven by ignorance and prejudice, that drives him to call the police, and this hurt Elias more than anything else. It serves to make him more sceptical of the Australian people and increasingly adamant that his family should not assimilate into the Australian way of life, he now absolutely forbids his children from having Anglo-Australian friends.

It is early Monday morning and Elias must head off to the markets so he can buy fruit and vegetables to restock the shop, the early rise is harder than normal because he has only had a couple of hours sleep. Normally when he gets back from the markets his parents help restock the shelves, but not today because Leila has a doctor's appointment. Nadeem will take her, and this means they will both need to leave early to get there on time. Elias is very worried about his mother; her health is failing, and this has been weighing heavily on his mind of late and likely added to his poor sleep last night. Leila reassures her son that there is nothing to worry about, but that does little to put his mind at ease. He has a terrible fear of losing his mother, they have gone through so much together and their bond is tight. Elias doesn't know a person in the world that understand him the way his mother does.

After what feels like the longest day he can recall, the afternoon rush finally winds down and Elias takes a quick break, by now he is exhausted. And so, today he has less patience than normal for the unruly kids that stop by at the shop each afternoon after school. As they do every visit, the kids move around his shop like a swarm of flies touching everything with their grubby little hands. They never buy much, usually just a packet of chips which they share. They dig their hands into the packet all at once desperate to get their share of chips, and inevitably leave crumbs all over the floor. This infuriates Elias because his poor mother gave the floors a good sweep and mop before leaving for the doctors.

After devouring the chips, they continue to swarm around the shop but this time one of the kids grab a packet of lollies and quickly hides it in his pocket. What they don't realise is that Elias has been watching their every move from behind the counter where he has taken a seat to rest his legs. He watches them like a hawk, money is money no matter how little, and he is not going to let them to steal from him. Normally he just takes the stolen item back and directs the kids out of his shop ordering them never to return. Today he has zero patience and quickly chases down the little thief and grabs him by the ear.

'You're a thief, take that packet of sweets out of your pocket and hand it back.' He demands.

The kids look surprised because normally Elias never touches them, just tries to scare the boys, but not this time, so the boy quickly returns the stolen lollies. Elias lets go of his ear and the boys run out of the store, fearful of Elias for the first time.

The day is almost over, and Elias can't wait until the end of trade, he has nothing left in him. As he counts the takings of the day, a tall heavy set man storms into the shop reeking of alcohol. He looks dishevelled and unkept, sporting a long dirty beard. He smells badly of an odour festering from his sweat drenched shirt, unlikely to have been laundered for a few days. Staring contemptuously at Elias with his beady little eyes, the ogre fires away spewing insults at him.

'What did you do to my son you dirty wog? You're not allowed to hit my kid, not in this country, only I can. Don't you know that filthy wog?' He screams at Elias spraying him with spittle and Elias wipes it off his face in disgust.

'Your son is a thief mate; he stole from my shop.' Elias retaliates.

'I'll call the cops if you touch my boy again.' He threatens.

'I'll call the police next time your son steals from my shop.' Elias stands his ground.

'Fucking wog, why don't you go back to where you came from?'

'If you don't leave my shop, I will call the police.' Elias has had enough.

The stranger seethes with fury and disdain and after a prolonged attempt to stare down his prey he gives in and leaves the store. Perhaps he is also already in trouble with the law and doesn't want to deal with the police.

Elias does his best to maintain his composure, but he is furious, he closes the store before making any rash decisions like chasing after the thug that just chastised him. He is terribly disheartened by the events of the day, disillusioned, and hurt by the appalling way Australian people have treated him and his family. For the first time he wishes he could go back to Lebanon, but the thought is fleeting. Reality sets in quickly because he knows he could never have accrued the wealth he has in this country, not even a tenth of what he has now could have been made back home in Lebanon. Even so his whole family lives here now, he couldn't leave them, especially his mother. Sadly, Elias becomes more detached from the Australian people and their way of life, he grows increasingly resentful of them. This serves to create a deep division between Elias and his children. With every day that passes the children identify more and more with the Australian way and far less with their father's culture.

A few years pass and the kids are growing up, Joseph is already in primary school but sadly seems to struggle with it. He has always been a shy and anxious child, unlike his confident and strong-willed sisters. He doesn't have any friends at school and is constantly getting picked on. He often gets stomach aches on the morning he has school but never on the weekend or during school holidays, and his parents don't see any connection between his nervousness and tummy complaints because anxiety is a completely foreign concept to them. Accordingly, Joseph always clings to his sisters at school when not in class, shadowing them around the playground. Mary insists that her daughters protect their little brother at school, and they happily oblige. In fact, Leila, Claudia, and Nada are extremely protective of Joseph and often threaten bullies with a fight if they pick on their brother.

At the end of each school day Mary waits in the schoolyard for the bell to ring so the children can be let out of class. As soon as Joseph sees his mother, he races straight up to her giving his mother a big hug, he smiles joyfully feeling a great sense of relief. From that point onwards he clings to his mother for the rest of the afternoon and evening, not allowing her out of his sight. Mary knows this is not how most children his age act, all the other boys reluctantly part with their friends when school ends and it's time to go home. Over the years she has tried to put it down to his quiet and shy nature and has swept her concerns under the carpet, but it is becoming difficult to ignore the possibility that something might be wrong. Elias on the other hand is critical of his son's clinginess, insisting no son of his should be like this, he expects Joseph to be physically and mentally strong. He resents that his son is weak whereas his daughters are confident and outspoken, he thinks it should be the other way around and blames Mary for raising the kids like this. Sadly, this just makes poor Joseph feel worse about himself and eerily it is just how Nadeem treated him as a child.

The school has invited Elias and Mary to a meeting with the principal to discuss some concerns they have about Joseph, and this worries Mary a lot because she is scared about what it could all mean. She wonders if there could be something very wrong with her poor boy, causing her to feel sick to the stomach with fear. Filled with dread she wonders if they might try and make Joseph go to a special school, she can't stop worrying. Elias on the other hand is annoyed about having to close the shop, his parents can't work today, Leila is not well again. All the school has told them is that Joseph cries excessively when kids pick on him, they think he gets upset about most things. Naturally this infuriates Elias and Mary who can't understand why the school is not addressing the bullying as the problem, not their boy. They both decide that this must be why Joseph doesn't like going to school.

Seated outside of the principal's office Mary and Elias wait to be called into the meeting. Mary fidgets anxiously in her chair, whilst Elias sighs angrily at the thought of wasting time here rather be in his shop making money. The principal finally emerges from his office to greet them, but he appears cold and detached, smiling superficially at the unhappy couple, his lack of warmth does little to put them at ease.

'Hello, my name is Mr John Skinner, I'm the principal, but just call me John.' He offers to shake hands with Elias, who ignores the gesture. Mary compensates for her husband's rudeness by smiling politely at the principal, aware Elias will likely only make matters worse by his actions.

'Come into my office Mr and Mrs Boutros.' He chooses to ignore the brush off.

Elias and Mary follow him into his office and the principal takes a seat behind his large desk creating a sense of distance between himself and his guests. He gestures for them to take a seat pointing at two uncomfortable wooden chairs opposite to where he sits. This seating arrangement merely reinforces the couple's level of discomfort.

'Thank you for coming in today, I don't want you to be concerned about this meeting. There are just a few things we've noticed about Joseph in the classroom that we want to discuss with you.' He explains in a matter of fact.

'I know he is being picked on, and I want to know what the school is doing about that?' Elias gets to the point of his concern and Mary nods in agreement.

'Mr Boutros, I understand you are upset but the kids pick on each other all the time, it's normal playground behaviour.' He defends himself.

'To call my son a wog is acceptable?' Elias questions the principal.

'There is no evidence that language has been used.' The principal asserts.

'Well, I believe my son, he says it happens every day.' Elias insists.

'Mr and Mrs Boutros I can understand that is upsetting and I will speak to all the teachers to watch out carefully for that kind of behaviour, you have my word. The reason I asked you to come to meet with me is because Joseph has become more and more withdrawn in class. He doesn't mingle with the other children and his language skills are not where they should be for his age.' He gets to the point.

'If he is being bullied, why would he want to mix with these children? And he speaks Arabic at home, English is his second language so of course he will be a little slower.' Elias asserts.

'With all due respect Mr Boutros, English should be his first language.' He looks puzzled wondering why anyone would think otherwise.

'Sorry Mr Skinner but Arabic is our first language.' Elias insists yet again.

All the while Mary has stayed out of this, but she can see the conversation is going around in circles as the two egos battle it out, and so she decides to intervene.

'Mr Skinner, what are you asking us to do?' She tries to bring the meeting back on track.

'We would like to recommend some assessments be undertaken by a psychologist, just to rule out any learning difficulties or emotional issues.' He informs them.

'What conditions? My son has no condition, this school is the problem.' Elias has had enough, and he gets up to leave. Mary looks distressed because the school may have a point, however the principal has all but given up.

'The school is merely suggesting this to help your son, it's up to you as parents to do something.' He explains.

'Come on Mary.' Elias has one foot out the door, totally fed up.

'We will think about it Mr Skinner, thank you.' Mary politely insists and hurries out of the office to catch up to Elias, who has by now already left the office altogether.

As the years pass Joseph's parents do nothing to address any of the concerns raised by the school. Although Mary did want to seek some advice from a psychologist regarding the concerns raised by the school, she was not prepared to fight that battle with Elias. Even so, she herself was quite sceptical about how a psychologist could help their son, and the school did little to try and explain the function and benefits of such a professional, perhaps that may have helped. Back in the village no one would even know what a psychologist did, let alone how they could help, and the school had no insight into this. The school catered to mainstream Australian culture, the concept of diversity and inclusion did not exist, you were expected to live and think like an Australian, no matter where you came from. Accordingly, the school had no idea that Joseph's parents might be suspicious about what this so-called psychologist could do for their son.

Regardless of how unhelpful the school proved to be there was another big reason why Joseph was never going to get the help he needed, Elias was way too proud to think there could be anything wrong with his son. Mary herself was too afraid to delve into something that terrified her, she dreaded the thought that there might be something wrong with her sweet boy. So, despite Joseph's inclination to stay in his room and keep to himself exceedingly, Mary chose to ignore it, too afraid to get to the bottom of what she kept telling herself was probably nothing.

Whilst Joseph causes his mother angst, Leila proves to be the opposite. She goes to a selective school and has done so for the past four years and even at a school full of high performers she continues to sit ahead of her year. Mary's grandfather was a doctor, and she thinks this might be where Leila gets her smarts from, it couldn't be from her in-law's lineage she is certain. Disturbingly Mary has no idea that Nadeem is not her husband's real father, it's something Nadeem has always insisted be kept secret. Shockingly, Elias has hid the truth from Mary for all their years of marriage, unwilling to mention anything, afraid of how his stepfather might react. Elias' grandfather by blood was meant to become a lawyer, but he got tied into running the farm instead, and so this could be the reason why Leila is so smart. Not just an intelligent girl, Leila is also very beautiful, she is the mirror image of her paternal grandmother.

Leila has been preoccupied lately; she is worried about telling her father about an overnight school excursion. The thought of asking him for permission to go to Canberra for two nights makes her so nervous she hasn't been able to sleep or eat much this past week. Mary has already told Leila she won't be able to go, there is no way her father will allow it. Although Mary has no issue with Leila going on the excursion, she knows what Elias will say, he would never allow it. Elias is aware of what his father and the community might have to say about any of his children spending a night away from their home.

Leila has kept putting off asking her father about the excursion for a month, but now she has to say something, the permission note is due tomorrow, and she has no choice but to muster up enough courage to ask him tonight. It's mealtime for Elias and he sits alone at the table eating his dinner. Even though the kids are older now and able to eat dinner with their father later in the evening, the habit of him eating alone has stuck. Even so, Elias likes it this way, it allows him to unwind after a tough day at work without having to talk to anyone. Knowing this, it makes Leila's job a lot harder, so she waits for him to finish his meal. He drinks his last drop of arak, and then leans back in his chair to relax. Leila thinks this will be her best chance to talk to him, so she bravely enters the room and sits down at the table. He smiles at Leila puzzled by her presence, nonetheless he is happy to see his clever daughter that fills him with such pride.

'How is school my clever daughter?' Elias asks Leila in Arabic. He refuses to speak English at home and expects that to be the rule for all the whole family.

'It's very good father, I'm top of my class even at the selective school.' She smiles at him.

'You are my pride and joy, so smart. Do you need something?' He asks.

Leila takes out the permission note and gives it to him as her hand trembles.

'Are you ok? What's wrong with your hand?' He asks with concern.

'Nothing, it's ok, maybe it's because I had coffee this morning.' She lies trying to throw him off. 'I have to go to an excursion for school and it's in Canberra.' She tells him filled with angst.

'That's a three-hour drive to get there and then three hours to get back? What a long day? Here give me the notice so I can sign.' He happily concedes.

'It's for two nights, we have to stay overnight.' She insists nervously.

Elias puts down the pen and stares at her in disbelief.

'Don't be stupid, you can't go then.' He laughs and pushes the note away.

'The whole class is going, what will I tell the teacher?' She bursts into tears.

'Maybe this is ok for them, the Australian families, but in our culture staying overnight away from your family is forbidden. We would be looked upon with disrespect, it's shameful Leila.' He tries to explain.

'I don't know what to tell the teacher?' Leila sobs.

'Tell them your father says you can't go, that's all.' He insists.

Leila knows there is no point trying to convince him otherwise and leaves the room in tears. Mary has been listening from the other room and is heartbroken for her daughter. She decides to at least try and convince her husband.

'You know she is a good girl,' Mary explains standing by the door nervously.

'Of course, she is, but what about the other children? These Australians don't have morals and I don't want them near our daughter.'

'They have teachers watching all the time and the girls and boys have to sleep in separate buildings.' She insists.

'What do you think the relatives will say? They will call her a slut, and this will bring shame on our family.' He stares at his wife surprised she doesn't get that.

'You are mainly worried about what your father thinks.' She has a go at him.

'I explained why already, don't cause trouble.'

'I don't want to lose our children one day when they decide we have been too strict. Look at you, your brother and sisters are strangers to your family.'

'Enough.' Elias yells at her. 'I want our family to be respectable and moral. This country does not have the same values and traditions as us. Now please leave me alone.'

Mary retreats out of the kitchen knowing she is never going to change his mind.

Five years on and Mary's precious little babies have grown up, the girls are all but adults, with Joseph not far behind. Leila is a second-year medical student at Sydney university, Claudia is in her first year at the same uni studying Accounting. Nada, on the other hand decided to leave school at the end of Year 10 to take up a hairdressing apprentice-ship, which she happens to love. Joseph is still at school and loathes it, he gets bad marks which makes him hate school even more.

He has begun to miss some classes at school and barely communi-cates with his family anymore, preferring to keep to himself in his bedroom. No longer the sweet shy boy that clung to his mother's skirt, he has become distant and cold, this breaks Mary's heart. She used to feel suffocated by his clingy ways but now misses it terribly, mother and son were always so close. She blames herself for his behaviour, perhaps she should have taken him to see a psychologist all those years ago. Mary doesn't realise her son adores her, but he doesn't want to be soft anymore, he struggles with this persona because he wants to fit in with a tougher crowd, his meek and kind true self doesn't cut it. As most teenage boys do, he wants to fit in with a group of friends but as it happens, he chooses the wrong crowd.

He has one friend, John who lives across the road, they have been friends since his family moved into the neighbourhood a few years ago. John is a lot like Joseph, shy and socially awkward, so they connect and can relate to one another. Unfortunately, the two boys have fallen into bad company of late, there is a gang that gather at the local shopping centre during the weekdays, and they have welcomed the two boys into their group, hence the reason for Joseph's absence from school. The gang have dropped out of school and use Joseph and John for their lunch money and to throw off police who see these two kids as harmless. Both boys are terribly naive and have no idea this is the reason why they belong to what they consider a cool gang. Both have started to smoke marijuana; the gang introduced the drug to them. Joseph feels bad about smoking because he knows it would break his mother's heart if she ever found out, but for the first time in his life he feels less anxious, the marijuana relaxes him. He also feels terrible about taking money out of Mary's purse to pay for it, he did think about taking it from his father's wallet but quickly realised he'd notice if any money was missing.

Mary dislikes that Joseph misses' school and loathes this new group of friends that he hangs with, it really worries her. She can't understand how this ever happened, her daughters were perfect angels in comparison. Sadly, Elias handles his son's defiance poorly, he resorts to beating him whenever he misses classes at school, it doesn't help at all, in fact it just makes Joseph resent his father more, causing him to act out further. Mary resents the violent approach her husband takes in dealing with this problem, she begs Elias to stop hurting their son, insisting it is only making matters worse. Elias refuses to soften, he must teach his son to be responsible and he believes this is the only way to do it. Mary begs Joseph to go to school, so his father won't hurt him, but Joseph doesn't listen.

Over the next couple of months Joseph goes from missing a few classes to many and finally the school takes a stand threatening to expel Joseph should he continue to miss this much school time. Elias cannot see any other way to manage Joseph other than through force, but this does nothing, rather is fuel his son's hatred for him. Mary becomes despondent, worried sick for her son's future and wellbeing. Elias doesn't worry as much about how Joseph's expulsion will affect his education and wellbeing, rather he is more concerned about how the community might judge him and the rest of the family.

One day Elias and Mary receive a visit from the police which surprises them, they can't think of any reason for it, Elias stopped making arak over a decade ago. Mary invites the two police officers into their home and Elias watches them sceptically, they have never been helpful to him whenever customers have stolen from his store.

'Does Joseph Boutros live here?' One of the officers asks.

'Yes, he is our son, why are you asking?' Elias demands to know.

'We have reason to believe he might be involved as an accomplice in a car theft.'

The couple look mortified, how could their son be involved in breaking the law they wonder in shock.

'That's stupid, my son would never do that.' Elias snaps outraged by the suggestion.

'Where was your son last night?' The officer asks.

'In his bedroom, what do you think?' Elias snaps. Mary knows her place and doesn't say anything.

'Is it possible he left the house without you knowing?'

'Impossible. I'm the last one to sleep at night, I would have seen him.' He insists.

'We will need to speak to your son, is he home now?' The officer asks.

'He is upstairs in his bedroom, tell him to come down here now.' Elias orders Mary.

She heads up the stairs just as Joseph appears looking very nervous. He walks down the stairs and approaches the police officers.

'We would like to have a word with your son, alone?' The officer insists.

'Yes of course, you can go into the lounge room.' Mary politely suggests and Elias does not look impressed, it's not her place to talk but Mary is desperately trying to keep the peace and he knows it.

'Would you like some coffee?' Mary asks them.

'No thank you.' They politely decline.

Elias and Mary leave the room so the police can speak to Joseph.

Half an hour later the police head back into the kitchen where Elias and Mary are sitting nervously awaiting the outcome of their interview with Joseph.

'We will let your son off this time because he really had nothing to do with the theft itself. I suggest you keep a close eye on him, or he will find himself getting into trouble, especially if he keeps hanging out with that group of boys. He's a good kid, just in bad company.'

'Thank you, we will definitely do that.' Mary politely obliges. Elias merely gives a cold nod to the officers.

After the police leave the girls emerge from their rooms and Joseph heads straight up to his. He doesn't get far as Elias lashes out at him. Sadly, Joseph cops a fierce beating and no matter how hard Mary tries to stop her husband, but he pushes her away each time, the girls watch in horror too afraid to step in.

Once Elias retreats into the lounge room Leila sneaks into her brother's room, careful that her father can't see. Joseph doesn't speak to her and Leila wonders what ever happened to that sweet shy little brother of hers. She takes out a first aid kit to tend to his wounds.

'I'm sorry he hurt you, Joe.' Leila says sadly.

He just shrugs his shoulders unwilling to talk. Leila finishes up and stares at her brother.

'I wish I could understand what makes you want to be with those boys, they are all going to end up in jail, is that what you want for yourself?'

Joseph shrugs his shoulders as he keeps his head down.

'We want to protect you, everybody loves you Joe,'

'He doesn't.' Joseph mutters under his breath.

'Of course, he does. He's just very old fashioned, tradition and culture are very important to him.' She tries to explain.

'Money is all he cares about and those stupid relatives.'

'No, his family is what he cares about.' She insists.

'Can you please leave me alone.' Joseph shuts her out.

Leila gets up to leave but before she goes, she places her hand gently on Joseph's shoulder staring lovingly at her brother, surprisingly he doesn't pull away.

The beatings do nothing to change Joseph's ways, it merely deepens his resentment for his father and the old fashion values he holds. Joseph does not understand his father's way of thinking, nor does he care to. He retreats into his own world, sadly a lot more trouble lies ahead.

9

Losing The One You Love

Several years later Mary finds herself bored and lonely at home with the children out and about most of the time. Her two oldest daughters spend much of the day at university, Nada works long hours to save enough money to buy her own hairdressing salon and Elias is at the shop from dawn to dusk. Although Joseph is at home most of the time, he rarely leaves his bedroom. Apart from cooking and cleaning Mary has no idea what to do with herself having spent more than two decades devoting herself to her children.

Despite his children's busy lives, Elias does expect the family to come together for a weekly extended family gathering at Nadeem and Leila's house. This happens every Sunday without fail and today is one of those days. And so, Elias, Mary, and the children, apart from Joseph, head over for the gathering on this warm Sunday afternoon. Elias has given up trying to fight his son into coming along to his grandparents' house, regardless of the beatings Joseph refuses to join them.

At the gathering all the women congregate in the kitchen to prepare a late afternoon feast of traditional Lebanese dishes. An oversized dining table is covered with plates of Lebanese delicacies such as kibbeh nayeh, a mix of raw minced lamb, cracked wheat and spices; kibbeh, a cooked variation of kibbeh nayeh with pine nuts added to the mix, shaped like tiny footballs, and then deep-fried; and barbecued skewered lamb, beef, and chicken slow cooked for hours, and that's just a few of the dishes. They busily prepare a variety of dips like hummus, a blend of chickpea soaked overnight, garlic, tahini, and lemon juice and toum, a strong creamy garlic sauce made from garlic, oil, lemon juice, and salt which leaves a stench on the skin for days. On top of that there are delicious salads including tabbouleh which is made from parsley, mint, tomatoes, burgher, and lemon juice and fattoush, a combination of fried Lebanese bread, lettuce, tomatoes, cucumbers, radishes, mixed in olive oil, lemon juice, garlic, salt. On top of all of that there is a mouth-watering assortment of baklava for dessert. Hours of cooking for hours of eating, an important Lebanese tradition.

As the women slave over the hot stove for hours the men congregate in the backyard to play backgammon, smoke their pipes, cigars, and cigarettes. They indulge in scotch and arak while discussing their prosperity and various marriages arrangements if that's what is required. The kids play carefree in the front yard away from the adults and their suffocating customs. They delight in fun games like marbles, hopscotch and hide and seek.

These weekly gatherings replaced the family time Elias, Mary and the kids had enjoyed together so many years ago. Those gatherings came to a quick end when Nadeem criticised his stepson for spending too much time with his immediate family, rather than with the extended family. Nadeem insisted that all the family should come together at his house, to strengthen the bond of the extended family in line with the culture and tradition of the old world. He remains highly critical of the Australian way of life which focusses on the nuclear family.

Later that afternoon Elias sits down with his parents to discuss plans for Leila's betrothal. Much to his daughter's annoyance they continue to pursue plans of her marriage to a third cousin. Leila is in her final year of university and will begin a medical internship the following year. She has no interest in marriage and wants to focus on her career. Elias is furious at his daughter's defiance while Mary could not be prouder of her daughter and so she defends her daughter's decision to become a doctor. This is a courageous stance that Mary takes, and she will endure tremendous backlash for it. The argument has already begun, and Nadeem takes the lead.

'You have no control over your children.' He scolds Mary. 'And you Elias, you should be tougher on Leila. What kind of woman chooses a career over marriage and children? It's a disgrace and an embarrassment to our family.' He yells at them in Arabic.

'She's very clever, why can't she be a doctor and marry in a few years?' Mary bravely asserts.

'Don't be ridiculous, who will marry her at that age?' Elias defends his stepfather.

'And what about Joseph? Where is he? People are laughing at your family, don't you see. This is embarrassing for me, not just you. You need to start controlling your children.' Nadeem does not hold back taking aim at Elias in particular.

Elias is so tired of the put downs, even after all that he has done to impress his stepfather, it all counts for nothing. Leila has heard enough and in an unusual act of courage she steps in to defend her son.

'Stop Nadeem, that's your son. He tries very hard. What do you expect from him when he has to work all the time. He is not the only parent.' Leila stares at Mary. Mary keeps her head down as she has already stirred the pot enough.

'The school ruined him.' Elias tries to defend himself.

'Both of your sisters don't have any of these problems with their children, stop making excuses. You need to control your wife more; she defends the children too much.' Nadeem criticises Elias. Mary has heard enough and gets up to leave.

'I think they are calling me to help in the kitchen, I better go.' She excuses herself and hurries off, desperate to escape.

'You need to control your family, this is not how I want our community to judge us, this is embarrassing for me.' Nadeem insists heartlessly. Elias looks away, beyond fed up with his stepfather and Leila watches on heartbroken for him. A thousand times she has wondered why she ever invited this beast of a man into their lives, surely being poor could not have been as bad as this.

Later in the evening Elias finally has an opportunity to speak with his mother in private. Nadeem has gone off to play cards with the rest of the male patriarch and he is well and truly drunk by now, Leila hopes that will be the last she sees of him for the evening before he passes out. Elias sits solemnly with his mother.

'You are going to be healthy again, the doctors say the medication is working.' He insists.

'I'm not scared of dying son.' She speaks frankly.

'Don't talk like that mother.' He begs. 'I can't imagine my life without you.' He stares at her overcome with sadness.

'Don't be silly my darling, we all come and go, no one lives forever. Soon I'll go and join the rest my family that went before me and one day the same will happen for you. This life is temporary, don't grow too attached to it.'

'Please stop mother, I know all of this but I'm not ready to let you go. Nobody has ever loved me the way you have.' He insists, deeply distressed. 'You have loved me so dearly, and protected me all my years, I can't imagine life without you.'

'I have had a full life son, it's different to the pain we faced losing our loved ones during the famine, they died too soon. But not me, it's my time, I have lived to be old.' She tries to convince him.

'Don't leave me alone mother.' He begs.

'Stop, you have a family that loves you. Mary is a good woman, and your daughters love you. Now Joseph, he is angry that is all, but he needs you. Spend more time with him, try to understand him.' Leila tries to make her son see.

'I think it's too late mother, maybe if I spent more time with him before, who knows? Maybe he has problems I have wrongly turned a blind eye to it, afraid of being judged if something was wrong, judged by every person here today, especially Nadeem.' Elias confesses.

'Nadeem is a pig and a mule, pay no attention to him. Speak to Leila, she is so smart, ask her if she thinks Joseph needs help. Be patient with your son, he needs you to love him.' Leila tries to make him understand. 'Look at how that awful man treated you.' Leila looks around nervously to make sure no one can hear. 'Still to this day he badgers you, he has been a horrible father to you, make sure your son is loved, don't make the same mistake.'

'I think it's too late; I have not been a great father, but he is a very difficult boy, I don't like to talk about it mother.' Elias says sadly. The conversation is too hurtful for him, so he shifts it in another direction.

'Leila is another headache for me. She wants to be a doctor instead of marrying and have children. I don't understand the children in this country, sometimes I just wish I could go back to Lebanon, where life was much simpler and more carefree.'

'I never wanted to come here but what choice did I have? How could I live without you and...' Suddenly Leila chokes up, she can't continue.

Elias holds his mother's hand and sits with her in silence.

'My heartbreaks whenever I think about Charbel and Nayla.' She sobs gently. 'My children, where are they? I want to know they are, ok? Before I die, I want to see them.' She begs tearfully. 'Not until I pass from this world will peace fall upon me, only then.' She stares intently at Elias.

'Don't make the same mistake as me, son. I lost two children because I never stood up to him. Don't let him influence you and cause you to push your children away.' She stares sadly at Elias, hesitating to go on afraid she might hurt him.

'You'll never make him happy my darling, never. Don't try to please him because you'll never be good enough for him, I never was. And don't be obsessed with money, what is most important are your children and our Father in Heaven, that's all, nothing else.'

Elias holds his mother's hand as she sobs, heartbroken for her.

Watching his mother breakdown over Charbel and Nayla the other night was heartbreaking, the thought of her not seeing them before she dies is gut-wrenching. Accordingly, Elias decides to make a genuine effort to seek out his estranged siblings. He can no longer bear watching his mother agonise over her losses, especially now that she is gravely ill. He doesn't care about the backlash he'll certainly face from Nadeem; he just wants to reunite his mother with Charbel and Nayla before she dies.

He begins his search by going to the factory Charbel worked at years ago, he hopes perhaps his brother still works there, and if he doesn't surely someone will point him in the right direction. Elias feels awful that he hasn't made this visit sooner. Had he pursued his brother's whereabouts earlier, much earlier, then his mother would have had many more years with her estranged children. Elias decides to stop by at the factory after the markets one day, he'll have to lose some hours of trade because he can't rely on Nadeem and Leila anymore.

When he visits the factory Elias is disappointed to find that Charbel hasn't worked there for quite some time, he retired a few years ago. The news hits Elias hard, not just because he is running out of time to find his siblings as Leila grows weaker, but also because so much time has passed. He can't believe that Charbel has retired, it only feels like yesterday that they were young men living in their tiny bachelor flat. He can't grasp how fast the years have passed; he is overcome by memories of some of the special times they spent together. There could have been more good times with Charbel if he tried to find him sooner, but he was too obsessed with pleasing Nadeem, seeking out his brother and sister would have certainly not helped that cause. There is some solace for Elias and his visit is not a waste of time, the factory foreman tells him that Charbel often visits to catch up with his old work mates. He promises to tell Charbel about the visit and will pass on Elias' contact details. Months pass and Charbel does not stop by at the shop, this troubles Elias because Leila is quickly deteriorating. He isn't surprised by his brother's decision not to visit, why would Charbel want to make any contact with a brother like him. He did nothing to support Charbel when he needed him most.

One late afternoon at the shop Elias feels tired after a long and busy day. He takes a load off and eases himself down onto his make-shift chair, a milk crate turned upside down. He begins to tally the daily takings and decides to call it a day. Without his parents helping in the shop, he works much harder and it's taking a toll on his ageing body, he is nearly sixty years of age. Claudia helps when she can but can't be relied on all the time, her work comes first.

Customers can't see Elias who sits below the steel countertop surface, but he can see them through the front facing countertop which is made from clear glass. He had the counter built like this to catch out any thieves that might try to steal from his shop while he sits hidden behind the bench. It also affords him privacy to eat when there is no body to cover him for a break. It has been an extremely busy day, so he hasn't eaten since the morning and is keen to close the shop and go home to eat his dinner.

Just as he finishes counting the takings of the day a customer enters the shop. Elias moans to himself because he was getting ready to close the shop. When he gets up, he can't believe what he sees, his dear brother standing there. They both stare at one another in shock unsure how to react, it's been nearly thirty years since they have spoken. Elias hurries around the counter to give his brother a hug, they hold one another tightly, overcome with emotion.

'How is mother?' Charbel asks anxiously in English.

Elias stares sadly at his brother trying to compose himself and Charbel reads him like a book.

'I must go and see her now.' Charbel insists in a panic

'Let me close the store first, before any customers come in.' He insists, speaking in English. He won't push the point of how important it is for them to speak in their mother tongue, not at a time like this.

Charbel looks upset and angry, saddened by all the lost years he could have spent with her.

'We can go and see her tomorrow.' Elias promises. 'I'll make us something to eat.'

'No, how can I eat? I'm worried, I want to see my mother.' Charbel insists, heartbroken.

'Father is there now, he'll cause trouble, please, it's not the right time. If we go now, it will only distress mother.' Elias begs him to see sense. 'We will go tomorrow first thing; can you contact Nayla so she can visit with us?'

'Yes, I will call her later.' Charbel sighs. He is completely unsettled; all he wants to do is see his mother.

'She's ok brother, she keeps asking for you and Nayla. Please don't panic, I promise you will see her tomorrow.'

'Then we will go tonight, after he leaves.' Charbel suggests.

'They won't let you in because of visiting hours.'

'I can't eat brother, I'm sick with worry.' Charbel insists.

Elias is starving because he hasn't eaten all day, but he won't eat in front of his brother, even if Charbel has no appetite. Elias closes the shop and hurries back to Charbel and takes a seat next to him.

'I'm sorry Charbel, for what I did to you.' Elias needs to get it off his chest.

'You never did anything wrong, our father did.'

'I could have tried harder to find you and Nayla.'

'And if you did, what would it matter? We were both banished from our home.' Charbel insists. 'What he did was wrong, Nayla and I have been separated from our mother and siblings for too many years because of him.'

Elias keeps his head down, knowing that he could have done more by arranging secret visits. He tries to shift the conversation because it is upsetting him.

'Do how is Hilda?'

'She's good, we have four beautiful daughters.' Charbel smiles proudly.

'God bless.' Elias smiles.

'And you?' Charbel asks.

'Three daughters and a son.'

'God bless, I would love to meet them.'

'Maybe you wouldn't, they are a headache for me.' Elias insists. 'They are not like us, there is no respect for our values, traditions and way of life.'

'They are your children; you have to make exceptions for the ones you love.' Charbel insists.

'No, they make my life very difficult, Joseph doesn't even talk to me.' He admits with a heavy heart, forgetful of all the reasons why Joseph won't speak to him. 'I don't have any control over him, sometimes I wish we never came to this country.' Elias shakes his head in silence.

Charbel stares at his brother with pity but doesn't know what to say. He has a wonderful family that he cannot complain about, although he paid a big price for it.

The brothers talk into the evening and when it gets too late, they call it a night, but agree to see one another the next day. Charbel and Nayla will get to visit their mother at the hospital, Elias just needs to make sure that Nadeem is not there.

Leila's condition has worsened overnight, and Elias is nervous that his brother and sister may not get to see their mother in time. He struggles to control his overwhelming emotions of both guilt and sadness. He should have brought Charbel here last night and punishes himself with thoughts of deep regret. As Elias sits by his mother's bedside watching her gasp for air, he wishes that it was him suffering right now, not her. She looks so gaunt, he knows not much time is left, she is only days away from passing or perhaps sooner.

Elias has arranged for his mother to receive end-of-life care in a private room, partly to accommodate visits from the large extended family, but mainly so she has as comfort and complete privacy at such a sacred time of her life. Unusually, he doesn't care that the private room is expensive despite his frugality, the deep love and respect he has for his mother means more to him than anything. Suddenly Leila begins to stir anxiously in her bed staring intently at the door.

'When will they come?' She asks in Arabic.

'Any time mother, I promise.' He tries to calm her.

'Maybe I'll die before then? Why did I let him push them away?' She sobs softly and weakly without any strength left in her.

'Please don't blame yourself, this was never your fault, no matter how many times I say it, you still blame yourself.' He insists.

He stares at this weak feeble woman who was once strong as an ox, she never gave up against all kinds of adversity, but now the only thing keeping her alive is the hope she'll see Charbel and Nayla one more time.

Suddenly the door opens, and Nayla enters with Charbel close behind, her prayers have been answered.

'Praise be to God'. She whispers to herself.'

Her banished son and daughter stare at their mother in shock, tears swell as they struggle to take this all in. When they last saw their mother, she was a picture of strength, healthy and full of life. Now she is a tiny figure of skin and bones with next to no life left in her. They hurry over to their mother and hug her, unwilling to ever let go again. She draws on all the energy left in her to speak as she gasps for air.

'My children I love you. I always loved you; I am sorry for what we did to you.' She coughs as she struggles to speak.

It's heart wrenching for them to hear, knowing this was never her fault, yet she blames herself. It was their father that robbed them of too many years and precious times they could have spent with their mother, a woman they love and adore so dearly. It is a bittersweet time for them knowing they have been afforded a chance to see her before she dies, but they have not seen their mother in decades! How could Nadeem have been so cruel? How could he have allowed his pride to cloud his judgement, to the extent that it tore their family apart.

Leila cries over the years she lost with Charbel and Nayla, time robbed from her by an awful man, a malice husband. Elias stares at his dying mother with deep sadness and regret, he blames himself for this, there was no reason why he couldn't have arranged secrets visits between his siblings and their mother. Or he could have stood up to Nadeem when he banished them from their home. Surely as the oldest sibling this would have been the noble thing for him to do, but he did nothing. Deep down he knows it was his selfishness that led to this horrible separation, he needed his stepfather's acceptance and received some of it when Charbel left. He will take this secret to his grave; how could he tell anyone the truth? He will never forgive himself for what he has done to his mother and siblings.

'Don't cry mother.' Nayla begs her, speaking in Arabic.

'I have devoted my life to God, He has given me strength, please don't be sad for me. I have been a nun for many years now, you can be proud of me.' She smiles at her mother through tears.

'Yes, I am proud of you darling daughter, for your great sacrifice in life, your devotion to God. Through your service to God, I will surely go straight to heaven.' She smiles at Nayla, suddenly calmer but still struggling to breath.

With all her strength Leila then turns to face Charbel. She smiles at him adoringly but has no energy to continue talking as she gasps for air. Charbel kisses his mother and stares at her adoringly.

'Mother, save your strength, don't be sad for me, I have a wonderful wife and four beautiful daughters.' Suddenly Charbel stops, choked up he tries desperately to compose himself; he won't allow himself to cry, that would merely add to her sadness.

'I will bring them to you tomorrow mother, I promise.' He forces a smile and Leila smiles back at him, giving a feeble nod. Charbel kisses his mother adoringly.

Leila begins to let go; she is much more at peace with her impending death now that she has seen her children. Her breathing grows very shallow, with creeping apnoea. Her children stand closely to their mother and watch her slowly slip away, filled with deep sadness they know she is approaching the end. When Leila takes her last breath, they don't know if that's it. They watch and hope she'll breath again like she has done for the last hour, but the breath never comes, she is gone. Leila has now passed leaving her children grief stricken and inconsolable. They hug and kiss her hoping their mother will wake up, such is the intensity of their shock and despair, they can't comprehend that she really has gone.

10
Lonely

Two years after his mother's passing, Elias remains profoundly sad, so crippled with grief he struggles to come to terms with her death. When Leila died, he buried himself into his work spending long hours in the shop desperate to distract himself from his painful loss. Be that as it may, this has only added further strain to his deeply fractured marriage. Elias is tired and cranky when he gets home from work and Mary is left to cook and clean for the whole family. Although the kids are out through the day working, aside from Joseph who continues to live like a hermit in his bedroom, they don't lift a finger to help when they get home, and their mother is left to do everything all on her own. Although Elias has never helped with chores as such, he used to at least force the kids to help their mother, now he doesn't even do that. All that aside, it has meant that Elias and Mary never have time to talk or support one another during these trying times.

Despite these challenges Mary's biggest struggle remains with Joseph who lives like a recluse. He spends all his time in his bedroom apart going to the bathroom or grabbing a meal from the fridge, which Mary always sets aside for him. He sleeps throughout the day so it's rare that anyone in the household ever sees him. Joseph dropped out of high school some time ago, but did commence an electrician apprenticeship, which he liked. Even so, he struggled with customer interactions, an inherent part of the job, being around people made him very anxious and after a while he began having panic attacks at work and eventually quit his job. Elias refuses to believe his son suffers from anxiety, rather he accuses him of using it as an excuse to avoid work because he thinks his son is lazy. Mary has no idea what a panic attack is, the condition is still not widely understood at this time, but she wants to help her son, she just doesn't know how.

With his parents all but giving up on him, they just don't know what else to do, Joseph falls into the traps of joining the realm of long-term unemployment, spending day and night in his bedroom, a place where he feels safe. He purchased a television with the money he saved from his apprenticeship and keeps it in his bedroom, this allows him to watch television late into the night and subsequently sleep throughout the day in his sanctuary. Leila worries that her brother is smoking marijuana, that is certainly what it smells like whenever she walks past his bedroom after working a nightshift at the hospital, but she doesn't draw any attention to it because it will cause trouble, besides she is not completely sure, she kids herself. Leila has her own secrets to hide, something that would surely break her father's heart.

She is deeply in love with her boyfriend Scott, a doctor and colleague from work, but she has kept this a secret from her family for nearly two years. Scott is Anglo-Australian, and Leila knows her father will disapprove of him, and most likely Mary will too. She knows her relationship with Scott will be seen as scandalous by the community and her family will be judged for it. To keep her relationship a secret Leila is forced to lie to her parents, so whenever she is with Scott, she tells her parents she is at work. Leila hates doing this and wonders how much longer she can keep it up.

Leila is spending the night at Scott's this evening, but she hasn't slept a wink. Laying wide awake in bed she feels terrible about lying to her parents, they think she is at work. She can't stop thinking about how on earth this relationship is going to work, she loves Scott but knows what will happen if her father finds out about them. She feels sick to the stomach for betraying them like this, what on earth would they think if they could see her right now? Leila doesn't think she is doing anything bad, or immoral as her father would certainly suggest, but she feels guilty for betraying them. Her father holds such old-fashioned values, he could never understand why she lives the life she does. Even so, she doesn't want to disappoint or hurt her parents as she loves them dearly. Leila respects them for all the sacrifices they have made over the years for their children, particularly providing for a good education. She knows about the poverty her father and grandmother experienced many decades ago and has seen how hard her father has worked in the shop to make sure his children never experience anything remotely close to that. Deep into her troubled thoughts, Leila doesn't notice Scott is awake now.

'You didn't sleep much again.' Scott insists, startling her. 'You have a fourteen-hour shift today, this is not good.'

'I know.' She sighs. 'The guilt of staying over plays on my mind and I can't sleep.'

'Why is this such a big deal? I honestly don't understand it. I'm a doctor, I come from a good family, and a wealthy family at that.' He insists, genuinely confused.

'You know that's not the problem.'

'Well then what's wrong with being an Aussie? Maybe you are worrying unnecessarily, they might surprise you.' He wants to give her hope.

'I really wish that was the case. You wouldn't understand if I explained it, it's so stupid the way they think.'

'What do they think?' He sounds offended.

'That I should marry a good Lebanese man, and if I don't it will be an embarrassment to the family.'

'That makes no sense.' He insists.

'I told you, it's crazy, and it makes no sense to me either. Look, I love you and that's all that should matter.' Leila tries to appease.

'What about our future together?' He pushes her.

'I will say something, I just need a little bit more time.' She smiles nervously at the man she loves. Scott is not happy, but he loves Leila, so he leaves the ball in her court, hoping she makes the right move.

The dilemma fills her with dread, Leila is aware of how angry her father will be if she tells him the truth. What if he follows in the footstep of his father and disowns her entirely, shuts her out in the same way that Nadeem did with Charbel and Nayla? In turn her poor mother will suffer terribly. She is being pushed to choose between her family and the man she loves and it's eating away at her.

When Leila finally musters up the courage to tell her parents about

Scott, Nadeem's health deteriorates and she decides that this is not be the best time to share her news, talking herself into waiting a little longer. Nadeem's memory has been failing him for a while, but he has only recently been diagnosed with Alzheimer's disease. Burying their heads in the sand, Nadeem's children have blamed his forgetfulness on old age for a long time, afraid to face the truth. His illness carries a lot of stigma in their community, and they don't want to tarnish his reputation or standing in the community. However, when Nadeem begins to wonder down the street half dressed, they must face the truth and manage his illness somehow.

Lately he has been roaming aimlessly around the streets with no insight into his whereabouts, often the neighbours must call the police for the sake of his safety. Despite the constant support from his children, the daughters in particular, Nadeem now needs around the clock care. Elias and his sisters are forced to decide about their father's living arrangements, but nobody offers to take Nadeem into their home. It's a big ask, not just because it will be tiring and time consuming but mainly because Nadeem is a beast to have around, the disease has not tempered his unpleasant nature, it has made it worse than before. Until a decision can be made about his permanent living arrangements Nadeem must move into respite care. Even with half his wits gone, Nadeem manages to control his children by refusing to go to a nursing home, his aggressive outburst, and insults guilt them into changing their minds. And so, they are left with a dilemma, unsure about who should take him in.

Charbel and Nayla have reconnected with the family since their mother's passing, albeit without Nadeem knowing it, his failing memory and confusion has allowed for a peaceful and effortless reunion. Even so, when Charbel offers to take their father into his home Elias objects, insisting that would be extremely unsettling for Nadeem should his memory momentarily returns, it would send their father into a fit of fury if he finds himself in Charbel's home. Everyone agrees it's not a good idea which is a relief for Elias, sadly there is still a covert fear of a rekindled relationship between father and son, no matter how unlikely, Elias remains threatened by Charbel.

Mary is outraged when she finds out that Elias has agreed to take Nadeem into their home without even mentioning it to her first. A reasonable objection by most, this is her house too, sadly Elias doesn't see it that way, he considers the house is his because he paid for it. Mary has argued with him for years about this, claiming he would never have been able to run a business without her, she practically raised the children on her own, cooked and cleaned without any help. She reminds him he would not have the money he has today without her support.

Their relationship is terribly fractured these days and Mary asks herself daily why on earth she married such a frugal and unreasonable man. Not only has she cooked and cleaned for this family for decades, now she must do the same for Nadeem and worst still she must watch him like a hawk. Mary has had enough and insists that Nadeem must at least spend weekends with either Zahra or Samya and Elias gives in, he knows he has pushed Mary to the brink.

Nadeem's move into their home is somewhat timely given Claudia will soon move out, much to Elias' delight she is set to marry Michael, a Lebanese Australian man highly respected within their community. He is a successful lawyer from a well-regarded family that has built substantial wealth since migrating to Australia. They both met at a wedding and Michael was instantly attracted to her, infatuated by her beauty, Claudia takes after her mother and father, she is blessed with good looks. The attraction is not mutual, but Claudia feels a lot of pressure from her father to marry and she doesn't want to disappoint him in the same way Leila has. Even so she is not ready to marry and has doubts about Michael, he is moody by nature, and this frightens her. Claudia divulges all her concerns about the impending marriage to her mother, naturally this worries Mary. She knows first-hand what can come from a rushed marriage, especially when her daughter is already having reservations. Even so, she knows what her husband will say if Claudia delays the marriage, the couple have been engaged for a year already. He will complain that she is getting old, already in her mid-twenties Claudia should be married with children by now, that is in accordance with their custom. Elias insists that Claudia has wasted enough time working post-graduation and it is time to marry and start a family.

Leila feels terrible for her poor sister and quietly guilty, but Claudia's impending marriage will take the focus off her. As the oldest, it should be Leila that is getting married but thanks to Claudia, her father has backed off for now. Leila continues to keep her relationship secret, and this also adds to her feelings of guilt. The couple have been together for over two years and Scott is not happy that he has yet to meet her family.

Nada works long hours in the hairdressing salon, still saving hard to buy her own business. She is already feeling the pressure of having to find a good husband and if she doesn't, Elias will find somebody for her. She is not interested in marrying a traditional Lebanese man because she resents the way her mother has been treated, she does not want to put up with what her mother has tolerated. For now, she is also safe and poor Claudia has her fate sealed and she couldn't be more worried.

With Claudia now married to Michael and out of the house, there is some room for Nadeem to move in, but it's not long before he causes a lot of chaos. Nadeem's condition has deteriorated to a point where he doesn't recognise or remember anyone in Elias and Mary's house, accordingly he accuses them of being intruders into his home. He frequently lashes out at the family which infuriates Mary, she often chases her father-in-law out of the house, fearing for her children's safety. Nadeem roams around the house watching everyone suspiciously, annoyingly he does this at night which keeps them all awake. Joseph is distressed by Nadeem's antics for different reasons, as a nocturnal person he can normally get to the kitchen for food at night and have his shower. Joseph dislikes any form of interaction with his grandfather and tries very hard to avoid him, sometime this means he must skip a meal or even go without a shower. With most of the family sleep deprived it doesn't take much time before one of them snaps, Mary has had the most to do with him, so there are no surprises when she is the first to lose it.

One morning Nadeem enters the house smiling as he carries a bucket of what he thinks is olives, he has only just picked them fresh off the tree. Unfortunately, the confusion from his illness causes him to mistake very small unripe lemons for olives. He has single-handedly ruined an entire tree of lemons that Mary was hoping to pick in a few months, and this causes her to fly off the handle.

'You idiot, why did you do that?' Mary yells at him in Arabic. Nadeem stares at her in confusion, he genuinely has no idea why she is angry at him.

'What's wrong with you, I picked all the olives for everyone. You should thank me you stupid woman, not insult me.' He screams at her in Arabic.

'These are lemons, not olives you fool. Those would have been lovely and juicy but now they're useless, you destroyed them.' She can't take much more so does not refrain from hurling more insults at him, and he does the same.

'Get out of my house.' He yells at her.

Leila hurries into the room after hearing the yelling from her bedroom, she watches in horror as the escalating argument unfolds. She feels bad for her grandfather knowing he has no idea he has done wrong but can also see how hard this whole living arrangement has been for her mother, she has carried the burden of watching him most of the time by virtue of being home all day.

'Mum, leave him alone. He can't understand what is happening, he's sick and you know that.'

Mary bursts into tears and slumps down into a chair. She is exhausted from the endless nights of poor sleep and can't take much more.

'Let me watch him, why don't you take a nap, you haven't slept much lately.' Leila kindly offers. Mary begins to calm down a little mopping up her tears with a napkin.

'You are a good girl.' Mary smiles at Leila through teary eyes. She gets up and heads off to her bedroom for a much-needed rest.

After hours of watching her grandfather's every move Leila takes a load off and sinks into a lounge chair. She can still see Nadeem wondering around and continues to watch him. Finally, he sits down next to Leila, and she thinks it's safe to relax. Exhausted from watching him and enduring nights of poor sleep Leila slowly doses off.

As she sleeps Nadeem springs to his feet and heads off into the kitchen because he is hungry and decides to fry up some eggs. He takes a frypan from the sink and pours way too much oil into it. He places the frypan full of oil onto the stove top and lights the gas burner using a cigarette lighter he took from Elias while he was sleeping. He goes to the fridge to gather some eggs but can't find any, and before too long Nadeem forgets what he is looking for and wonders off into another room, forgetting about the burning oil on the stovetop. Thankfully Elias has installed a fire alarm in the kitchen, fearing something like this might happen and the high-pitched screeching sound of the alarm snaps Leila out of a deep sleep. She instantly smells the burning oil and rushes into the kitchen to find the frypan engulfed in flames. She quickly puts out the flames with a fire blanket her father bought, again anticipating the dangers they face with his father living in their house. Leila then sets off to find her grandfather before he can cause any more damage somewhere else in the house. She tells her parents about the incident that night and Mary flies off the handle.

'He needs to go.' Mary yells at Elias, whilst her manner is untypical, she is fed up. 'Either you shut the shop and look after him yourself or he has to move in with one of your sisters.' She demands in a way her husband is not used to.

'That's my father you are talking about, don't be disrespectful. How can I shut the shop; I make money for us by working.'

'You make money for yourself. When do you ever spend money on us? You are getting old now, why do you even work when you don't need to?' She bursts into tears.

Mary has hit a brick wall; her marriage is not a happy one, but she knows the option to leave is not on the table. Leaving her husband would be shameful, even her parents would disapprove, despite how much they dislike Elias. Leila watches on feeling absolute pity for her mother, knowing that she does not deserve this.

'I'll talk to Zahra; she has a spare room.' He tries to appease his wife; he can see she is at her wits end and knows he must do something. Mary nods, surprised at Elias for showing some compassion.

Just when everyone begins to settle Nadeem is back at it again. As Nada enters the house after a long day at work, Nadeem begins to yell at her.

'Get out of my house you slut, I'll call the police.' Nadeem screams at Nada. Elias hurries after him and tries to calm his stepfather down. He stares at him with sadness, heartbroken by what this disease has reduced him to, he was once strong and proud and now he is none of that. Incredibly, and just for a moment, Elias forgets the cruelty this awful man inflicted on the whole family, and most of all him.

The next day Nadeem is all packed and ready to go with no idea he is moving in with his daughter Zahra. He sits comfortably in a lounge chair wondering why two large suitcases sit at the front door, Mary packed his belongings the moment Zahra agreed to take him off their hands. It is a Sunday so the whole family is home, a small comfort to Elias at a time he needs it, although he'd never admit that. He is feeling down, sad to see his stepfather being carted off to yet another home. Staring through rose-coloured glasses he momentarily forgets how horrible Nadeem treated his family, most of all him. Even so, he struggles to watch a once strong patriarch be reduced to this helpless and pathetic man with no insight into what has become of his life, for a brief and frightening moment he wonders if this could be him one day. He continues to struggle with the loss of his mother, it has been years now since her passing, but the raw grief still plagues him like it was just yesterday.

Oblivious to all that goes on around him Nadeem pulls out a pipe from his pocket, although filled with tobacco it's unlit and he inhales regardless. Feeling sorry for his stepfather, Elias walks across the room and sits next to him and lights his pipe. He sits close to Nadeem and watches him like a hawk, careful to avoid any further near miss fires. Elias is puzzled by the smell of smoke that flows from Nadeem's pipe; the strange scent doesn't smell like tobacco.

Nada walks into the room and instantly picks up that the strange scent of smoke is marijuana, and so she swiftly pulls the pipe out of her grandfather's mouth, unfortunately this just causes him to lash out at her.

'You thief, you witch.' Nadeem screams at her.

'That's marijuana he is smoking, where did he get it from?' Nada asks her father.

Suddenly filled with rage, Elias springs to his feet and races straight upstairs towards Joseph's room. Leila gets up quickly and chases after him worried for her brother's safety. Mary also runs behind after them, terrified by what he might do to Joseph.

'Leave him alone.' Leila pleads with her father. 'It's mine, not his.' She lies whilst trying to keep up with him, he is surprisingly quick for a man of his age. He calls Leila bluff ignoring her and charges into Joseph's room to find him fast asleep.

'Get up you no-hoper.' He yells loudly.

Joseph awakens, still half asleep and drowsy, and doesn't anticipate his father's attack as he pulls his son out of bed. Leila and Mary try desperately to pull him away from Joseph, but he is too strong.

'How dare you smoke drugs in this house. You disrespectful piece of shit, you should be ashamed of yourself. Get out of my house now.' He screams at Joseph. He leaves the room in a state of fury and Leila tries to comfort her brother as Mary cries inconsolably.

'It's alright mum, don't cry, I'll be ok.' He tries to console his mother. Mary looks shocked hearing him speak, he hasn't spoken to her in years, and now she sobs even harder.

'You can't go son, where would you live?' Terrified for his safety.

Leila stares hesitantly at her mother afraid to share what she believes is a solution to this problem, she knows it will break Mary's heart. For Joseph's sake she must make a call that will drag the family's reputation through the mud, but there is no other choice.

'You can come with me Joseph; I will take you somewhere and he'll never be able to lay a hand on you again.' She speaks softly to him.

'No, you will both stay here, this is my house too, he can't make Joseph leave.' Mary insists deeply distressed.

'I can't live here anymore either mum, it's too difficult having to follow his ridiculously strict rules.' She confesses careful not to give too much away.

'No.' Mary bursts into tears. 'Stop talking like this, I will speak to your father, he's angry right now, he'll change his mind.' Mary pleads with her.

'I can protect Joseph this way, it's cruel the way he treats him.' Leila insists.

Mary is broken, her children are the only light and hope that she has in this dark and sad life of hers. Leila tries to console her mother with a hug, but Mary stiffens like a board, how can Leila do this to her.

'Will you come with me Joseph?' Leila asks.

Joseph nods nervously, this is a terrifying step to take but he has no choice.

'How will I pay rent?' Joseph asks.

'I have a friend we can stay with.' She insists, leaving Scott's name out of it, that revelation will be too much for her mother to handle right now.

Mary has been deeply heartbroken since Leila and Joseph left a year ago, Elias pretends not to miss them and festers over the embarrassment their actions have caused for his family. The transition out of home has not been easy for Leila and Joseph either. In the beginning Leila and Scott really struggled with having Joseph live with them, his behaviour was deeply troubling. Leila always knew that her brother's reclusive behaviour was not completely her father's fault but realised that the abusive parenting didn't help either. She understood that there were other factors at play, specifically underlying emotional and psychological problems.

When Joseph first moved in, he continued to sleep throughout the day and watch television the whole way through the night. He never went anywhere at night, just stayed in his bedroom, only leaving to get food or to go to the bathroom. On the rare occasion that Leila did see him, mainly when she worked late, he barely spoke to her and quickly retreated into his bedroom. She gradually came to understand Joseph's room was his haven, a place where he could avoid interactions with people which caused him extreme anxiety. Leila insisted for months that Joseph should seek help from a professional, but he refused to do it. She let it go for a while but knew this was not going to help her little brother, in the end she threatened to send him back home, knowing she'd never really do it. Even so, for his sake she had to take drastic measures and threatened to send him back unless he agreed to get help, he consented to get help.

Unlike her father, Leila has always been very generous with her money, and so she spent whatever it took to get her brother properly assessed for his condition. After months of assessments, he was diagnosed with mild Autism and chronic anxiety disorder. Finally, there was an explanation for his longstanding issues, a problem that had crippled him with fear for many years. Leila became hopeful that there was a way forward for her brother, a chance for him to live a better life. She paid for all his sessions with the clinical psychologist and other health professionals and thankfully over time Joseph responded well to the therapy.

Now, in just a year since moving in with his sister, Joseph has a job and sleeps much better at night. He still experiences anxiety but knows how to manage it and even has a couple of new friends. Finally, his condition no longer restricts his ability to lead a normal life. Leila sees happiness in her brothers face for the first time in years, he hasn't smiled like this since he was a very small child when the nervousness began to creep into his life. If only Elias had swallowed his pride and sought professional help for his son, perhaps Joseph would not have suffered for as long as he did.

Scott has never come across anybody like Leila before, someone so selflessly dedicated to her family. He respects her deeply and is in awe of her kindness and commitment to her brother, it certainly isn't something his family would do. Scott knows how sad Leila has been since leaving the family home, and this weighs heavily on his mind. To appease Elias, Scott asks Leila to marry him hoping that will help lift some of the stigma their living arrangement has created. Leila refuses to marry for the wrong reason, besides she doesn't have the heart to tell him that getting married would not solve anything, the problem her father has with Scott is that he is not Lebanese.

It's sadly ironic that whilst Elias remains deeply critical of Leila's relationship, she is happily in love; on the other hand, whilst he approves of Claudia's marriage, she could not be more miserable in her loveless relationship. To make matters worse Claudia is already expecting her first child in the next month, and after just a year of marriage, worst still she will be bringing her precious baby into an extremely unhappy home. Claudia wanted to delay having children for another year or two for the sake of her prospering career, but Michael objected, insisting she had no need to work. He earns a good income and reminds her constantly and wants her to stay at home to raise their family. Michael refuses to believe Claudia enjoys working and wants a career, he can't imagine any mother would want to be away from their child for the sake of a career. He also reminds her of the stigma working mother's face, from their community. And so, very early on in their relationship alarm bells ring and sadly Claudia is too afraid to act.

On this night the alarm bells are deafening, heavily pregnant and tired after a long day at work Claudia is left to cook the evening meal and clean afterwards, meanwhile Michael lounges on the couch with his feet up reading the daily newspaper. Claudia's legs and back ache from the extra weight she carries this late into her pregnancy, so she rubs deep into her lower back hoping to alleviate some of the pain.

Finally, Michael gets up and Claudia looks relieved hoping he might take over for her, but he heads straight to the fridge and grabs a beer. She looks quietly disappointed but bites her tongue careful not to aggravate him.

'Oh, what's up now?' He groans as he snaps at her.

'Nothing.' She lies.

'Bullshit, what is it now? All you ever do is complain.' He unjustly criticises her.

'Nothing, I'm fine.' She tries to calm him.

'I don't understand it. I work bloody hard, and you make me feel like I can't take a load off after a long day.' He continues the attack and Claudia tries her best not to react.

'All you ever do is complain, I'm sick of it.' He continues to provoke. But this time Claudia has had enough.

'I work too, and my back aches with the baby coming, it would be nice if you could help with the dishes, that's all.' She instantly regrets her words knowing this will certainly set him off, and it does. He stares contemptuously at her and then spits right in her face. Claudia doesn't look shocked; this happens all the time. She wipes her face as she begins to move away from him anticipating the imminent beating which usually follows. She hurries out of the room and manages to break away despite the weight she carries, and then shuts the door closed on him. Running out of the house she tries desperately to reach her car before he catches up, but he is close on her tail and it's too late. She can suddenly feel the grip of his hands around her neck, and she knows she is in for a terrible beating tonight, her heart sinks. He drags her back towards their house and as they approach the front door a porch light from across the road illuminates and he quickly releases his grip.

'Get inside the house now and I won't hurt you.' He threatens. Terrified, she obliges and Michael places his arm around her waist leading her back into the house. She has defied him and will pay a terrible price.

Just as they enter the house, he slams the door shut and pushes her to the ground, Claudia wonders if he even thinks about the safety of their unborn child. The light across the road turns off leaving her all alone to fend for herself. She sobs feeling terrorised by this monster and her body shuts down as she endures her punishment. Like so many nights he beats her savagely and she accepts the agonising pain until he has finished. Once he leaves the room, she cries hysterically worried sick for the safety of her baby. He kicked her everywhere, but she shielded her stomach with her arms and legs and hopes and prays this was enough to protect her baby.

Claudia has endured this ongoing of abuse for the past year, attempting to leave Michael many times by going back home to her parents, but Elias has always sent her back begging his daughter not to provoke Michael so he will leave her alone. Mary fights tooth and nail with her husband pleading for him to let Claudia come back to the safety of their home, and to protect the wellbeing of her unborn child. Sadly, he is more worried about what the relatives will say if she comes back home. What would the community think about their pregnant daughter leaving her husband, a good respectable lawyer. All Elias can do is threaten to get the police involved, but Michael calls his bluff, he knows Elias would never do it, aware that Elias won't want to risk tarnishing the family name.

The following day Michael fusses over Claudia and cooks her breakfast, but she sees right through his sickening attempt to play down what happened last night. Even so, she still goes along with it terrified that if she doesn't that will ultimately lead to more violence. It's a pattern she knows too well, he picks a fight with her, beats her up and then apologises the next day promising it will never happen again. This cycle of abuse sickens her to the core, but she can't see a way out, she's tried to leave but has nowhere to go. Elias begs her to stay and try and avoid him when he's drunk, and in that way keep the peace. He can't permit her return home, he is too afraid of the consequences, Claudia is stuck. At a time when she should be overjoyed by the impending birth of her child, she is terrified and depressed.

There is another option for Claudia, but she refuses to consider it. Leila has begged her sister to leave Michael and come live with her. Claudia won't do it, as much as she loves Leila, she considers her living arrangement immoral. Claudia is far more traditional than her sister, she thinks Leila should not be living with a man out of wedlock, and so she won't move in with her, regardless of the danger she faces staying put. Like her father, she worries about how she and her unborn child will be judged by the Lebanese community. By moving in with her parents she would be judged as shameful, but by living with Leila, that would be downright scandalous. It's astonishing that despite this being the 1970's, a time of extreme social and cultural change, the clan that left Lebanon in the forties and fifties have held on tightly to the customs and traditions of the old country. They have preserved the same values they left with decades ago. And so, Claudia cannot return home or move in with Leila, not even for the safety of her unborn child.

When Michael finally leaves the house for work, he hopes he has done enough to placate his wife, fool her into thinking this will never happen again. In his sickened mind he truly believes that if she does not provoke him there will be no reason to get angry, leaving him no reason to touch her. Claudia knows the slightest thing will provoke this beast, but she has nowhere to go, and so the cycle of abuse continues.

With Michael gone for the day Claudia finally relaxes, at least for now. As always, following these traumatic beatings she sets about concealing her injuries as she applies makeup to all the visible bruises and lacerations that clothing can't hide. Her arms and legs are black and blue, she used them to shield the baby. She hurries to get ready for work, already running late because she can't find large enough clothing to wear. Not only does she struggle to find suitable clothing to accommodate her extra-large size, that is typical in the last month of pregnancy, but there is the added issue of finding something that will cover up all the lacerations and bruising. She knows that taking a few days off from work will allow time for the injuries to heal, but work distracts her mind and that's what she needs right now.

In the end she successfully covers up most of her wounds with the long sleeve dress she digs up from deep within her wardrobe, adding thick black stockings to completely disguise her injuries and now she is ready to head to the front door. She is startled when the doorbell rings, her heart beats fast and she collapses into a state of panic wondering who could be at the door. She dreads the thought that maybe a neighbour heard the beatings last night and wants to come and help, knowing how useless their efforts would be. The doorbell rings again so she has no choice but to go and answer it. Taking a deep breath, she opens the door only to find Nada standing there, suddenly Claudia feels a deep sense of relief. At first glance Nada can see Claudia has copped another beating and her blood begins to boil, she is furious. Nada knows the signs well, the clothing choice her sister makes to disguise the wounds and heaped on concealer. She barges into the house and looks around for the perpetrator ready to strangle him with her bare hands.

'He's not here.' Claudia snaps. She knows her little sister can't save her, nobody can.

'That dog! I'll kill him, I will Claudia. This must stop.' She struggles to hold back tears.

'I'm fine, just stop it, please.' Claudia tries to calm her sister. Nada can't believe what she is hearing.

'You are about to give birth and that monster still beats you. How do you stay here?' Nada can't comprehend. Suddenly Claudia unleashes her pent-up rage.

'What choice do I have?' She screams at her sister. Tears stream down her face which is now red with rage.

'Claudia.' Nada cries out. 'I won't let you do this to yourself.'

'What can I do?' She sobs.

'You are coming with me. I'm packing your stuff and you are leaving.' Nada won't take no for an answer.

'Are you mad? Listen to how crazy you sound?' Claudia challenges her.

'What about you? You're about to bring a child into the home of a crazy man. You can't do that!'

Claudia sobs inconsolably because she knows Nada's right, but she genuinely can't see a way out of this. Nada hugs her sister trying to calm her, they hold each other tightly, completely broken.

'We can stay at Uncle Charbel's, I know he will take us.' Nada pleads.

'What would dad say? That's crazy. Then he'll stop talking to his brother again, that's not fair.' Claudia insists.

'What about Leila? She'll take you. It's only for a while. I'll get a place and you and I can live together. I'll help with the baby, I promise you. I have a good job; I can pay the rent for as long as we need.'

Claudia is incredibly moved by her sister's kindness and generosity. But how can she convince Nada she's considered all options and there is no way out.

'I can't stay with Leila.'

'Please Claudia, I know you disapprove of her, but this could be a matter of life or death, this is not just about you, there's a baby to think about. Only for a month, just give me a month so I can get us a place.' Nada begs.

Claudia can't stop crying because she knows Nada's right, she must protect her baby. Nada stares desperately at her sister, hoping she will see sense in all of this.

'Dad won't talk to us anymore, you realise that.' Claudia tells her sister firmly as she wipes her face soaked in tears.

'You have no choice, Claudia. Is this the life you want for your child?' Nada begs again, and Claudia trembles with fear knowing Nada is right.

'Ok.' She agrees sighing nervously, she's sick with fear. Please let's just do this now before I change my mind.'

'You sit down, and I'll grab your bags. Just tell me what you need to have packed. You can't take everything, just the essentials.'

'Ok.' Claudia pauses. 'Thank you, Nada.' She smiles sadly at her.

'Thank you for being brave Claudia.' She tries to keep it together, so distressed by what her sister has had to endure.

Claudia's decision to leave Michael is terrifying to say the least, and with good reason because the escape is riddled with danger. When she finally leaves, he does everything humanly possible to hunt her down. As a well-regarded lawyer he has contacts everywhere and a good private detective is an easy find, in less than two weeks he knows where she is living. From that point onwards Michael stalks Claudia daily threatening to kill her unless she comes back home. The daily threats are harrowing, and it plays on her mind day and night, she can't eat or sleep. Worst of all, she knows the lack of sleep and constant worry is not good for her unborn child, she is due any day now. She must stay strong and thanks God for Nada and Leila; without them she probably would not have survived. For many months the thought of taking her own life seemed a far better option than the abuse she was suffering, if she had not moved in with Leila to escape him, she may not be here today.

Leila stays with her sister day and night taking a month off from work to do it, potential career suicide for a doctor in training, but she must protect her sister. Claudia is overcome with guilt knowing she has judged her sister poorly, she can now see how wrong her father has been, the narrow thinking caused him to lose his family, not preserve it. The fear of being judged and the impending banishment from the community that comes with it is just not worth it she finally accepts. Claudia wishes her father could change his thinking but knows that will most likely never happen, but at least she sees things differently now. She still loves her father despite all the bad things he has done and feels sorry for him knowing the pain he hides, the hurt stemming from years of abuse at the hands of his stepfather. She witnessed first-hand the cruelty her grandfather Nadeem directed at her father; she angrily watched him dish out constant unreasonable criticism that Elias did not deserve. Her grandmother Leila also told her sad stories about her father's upbringing in Lebanon, only when Nadeem wasn't around of course. Accordingly, unlike her other siblings Claudia has a soft spot for her father, and so when her baby is born, she names him after her father, Eli, short for Elias. The choice of name comes as a complete shock to her siblings, but she is proud to name her son after her father.

Scott begins to feel the strain of Leila's clan taking over their home and begs her to do something about it. Her solution is for the couple to purchase their first home, a house large enough to fit all her siblings and Eli. Scott is baffled by this decision but backs off out of love for his kind-hearted and selfless Leila, knowing how much she loves her family. Although Claudia is deeply grateful for all the help Leila has kindly provided, she wants a place of her own, a crying baby is going to be too stressful for the rest of the household. Thankfully Nada delivers on her promise, and she finds a flat for Claudia, Eli, and herself to move into, Joseph stays put with Leila and Scott for now. Claudia hopes that this will also throw Michael off their trail, unfortunately that is not to be.

Claudia has continued to endure sleepless nights worrying about what Michael might do next, at least now she can feel safer because they live in a high security building, poor Nada pays heftily for it but won't have it any other way. As it turns out, Michael's next move is more terrifying than his first threat, he launches a legal battle for full custody of Eli. Instead of enjoying her gorgeous newborn son, Claudia must fight tooth and nail to keep her child safe from the clutches of this crazy man. Unfortunately for her, Michael knows the law inside out and she can't afford a good lawyer to defend herself. She stopped working when Eli was born and so has no income, this has left her in a state of constant panic.

Leila and Nada have decided to pool together all their savings to pay for a lawyer, but Claudia won't take their money. She is overwhelmed by their kindness but can't accept their money, who knows when they might need it. Despite all the bad things her father has done, Claudia can see he has had a hand in the way his siblings turned out. Growing up her father always pushed his children to respect and value family, to help one another no matter what. Granted Mary drove those values even harder than her husband.

Scott has always been in awe of Leila's kindness and devotion to her family and wishes his own family could be a more like that. With that in mind he goes to see his brother, a notable barrister and asks him to represent Claudia for free. In return for the favour Scott promises to provide his brother and his family with all the free medical advice they might need in the years to come. And so, in the end Leila and Nada don't need to beg Claudia to take their money because Scott's brother agrees to represent Claudia for free.

When the case goes before the family court Claudia wins easily, she is granted full custody of Eli. Her lawyer provides a convincing factual account of all the gruesome beatings and threats Claudia endured throughout their marriage, persuading the magistrate with no difficulty that Claudia's husband is completely unfit and incapable of providing a safe home for Eli. Claudia immediately applies for an apprehended violence order against Michael, in doing so she can protect herself and her son from any potential acts of violence, intimidation or harassment. Michael ends up lying to all their community about Claudia, painting himself as the victim. Claudia lets it go because she is already an outcast for leaving her marriage, she just wants Michael out of her life. Finally, she can breathe easy.

All the while poor Mary is devastated by the exodus of her children, the only true source of happiness in her life has vanished, her children kept her going in a very unhappy marriage. Claudia feels awful about her poor mother's situation and decides to visit one day when Elias is at work.

In one visit Claudia manages to sweep away all the darkness in Mary's life. Her mother can't stop smiling at the sight of her darling baby grandson. Hours pass quickly and Claudia needs to leave soon, she knows her father will be home shortly. Mary begs her daughter to come back the next day and Claudia will make all the effort to, but to play it safe she explains the bus route system to her mother hoping she can come to her place instead. In this way Claudia can keep her son in a good routine, plus hopefully Mary will get to see Nada as well.

Since moving out the children have tried to drop by and visit their mother whenever possible, but they are still afraid that their father might come home from the shop unannounced, it's an unrealistic fear but very real for them. Mary knows that if she wants to see her children and her precious grandson, she will need to go to them. She hopes that her husband never finds out, but she refuses to miss out on spending time with her children and her darling grandson.

And so, each day, Monday through to Friday, Mary embarks on her secret visits to see Claudia and Eli. She leaves her house the moment Elias' car vanishes down the street, as he heads off to work. She spends most of her day with Claudia and Eli and then comes home just in time to prepare a meal for her husband hoping he doesn't catch on to what she has been up to through the day. Mary occasionally sees the rest of her children on the days they don't work, it's not often enough but better than not seeing them at all. Every time Elias asks for Mary's help in the shop she turns him down, insisting she hates the shop and that he should sell the business. She gets nervous that perhaps he will do as she suggests and that will bring an end to her visits, but then quickly realises money remains very important to him so he would never walk away from the shop willingly.

It is not too long before Elias suspects something strange is going on with Mary because she is a lot happier these days, her depressed mood that manifested after the children left has lifted. And so, he decides to see what she is getting up to by parking his car down the bottom of their street one morning instead of heading off to work. This will cost him business by opening the shop later, but he is puzzled by her change in mood and nervously wonders why. He waits impatiently in his car for what feels like hours but is much less.

And so, Mary thinks Elias has gone to work and quickly gets ready to leave the house for her daily visit. He is taken by surprise when he notices Mary leaves the house, and then walks briskly down the street toward the bus stop. He wasn't paranoid after all; she really is up to something, and he has no idea what that could be. He swiftly turns the engine on and does a U-turn heading quickly down the street in her direction. When he sees a bus approaching the bus stop, he blows the horn before Mary gets a chance to alight the bus. Startled by the loud honk, Mary looks up to see why someone is blowing their car horn, her heart skips a beat when she sees that it's her angry husband and doesn't know how she will get out of this.

Mary decides she must tell him the truth, so he knows she is not up to something sinister, like visiting someone outside of their community. She confesses, telling him all about her precious visits to Claudia and Eli. Surprisingly Elias doesn't get angry, rather he wants to know everything about his baby grandson, although hoping not to come off too excited. Not seeing his grandson eats away at him, but his pride gets in the way, it prevents him from reconnecting with Claudia and in turn meeting his grandson. Elias has become more and more like his father, overly concerned about what the community thinks, rather than seeking out what really makes him happy. He is beginning to stare down the barrel of a lonely existence, facing the prospect of growing old alone. Of course, he has Mary whom he loves, although he has a strange way of showing it, but he is missing his children, and now his grandchild. He is hurting deeply at the thought of never seeing them again, but far be it that he would ever admit to that. He is happy for Mary to continue with her visits insisting that she conducts herself discreetly, making every effort to ensure nobody from the community ever finds out. She happily complies, surprised that her husband does not put an end to her visits. She wonders how on earth she can convince this terribly stubborn man that he must reach out to his children, to pave the way for a reunion with the ones he loves.

Mary's connection with their grandson means he gets to hear all about how Eli is doing following her daily visits. This provides a glimmer of happiness following the dark days that have plagued him since the death of his mother, sadly this joy is short lived because he receives word that Nadeem is seriously ill and has been admitted into hospital with pneumonia and a failing heart. It is strange that Elias feels sad about this, after all those years of torment. Perhaps he is disheartened by the possibility that this is how he will end up in the years to come, a lonely old man.

He goes to see his stepfather at the hospital each day after work, it helps to distract his mind from the feelings of loneliness left buried deep within him the day his mother died. He still finds the visits depressing though because Nadeem doesn't remember his family anymore, he yells feebly at them when they come to see him, even when Charbel and Nayla visit Nadeem has no memory of them. He is now a frail old man with not much fight left in him. Elias stares sadly at the shell of a man that was once a powerful patriarch, admired by all his family, relatives, and community.

Even so, he hasn't forgotten how cruel his stepfather had been, the memories are raw and not swayed by the image of a feeble old man lying on his deathbed. To this day Elias fights demons deep within him, the terrible memories of the past never leave him. He tried his best since very young to impress his stepfather, but it never helped, all he ever hoped for was love and pride from this old man. He spent all his adult years trying to win him over but deep down always knew he fought a losing battle. Nadeem would never see Elias as his own, he simply wasn't of his blood. Yet Elias sacrificed everything to try and make his stepfather proud, sadly that included pushing his own children away. At this dark moment he wishes he could turn back the clock and try things differently, but it is too late. He has become just like Nadeem and will grow old and lonely just like him, loathed by his family. A few days later Nadeem passes with none of his children by his side.

Since Nadeem's passing Elias has struggled to feel motivated about anything, he doesn't even have his heart in the business anymore. This is an unusual turn of events for a man who poured his heart and soul into his shop for more than four decades. For the first time since his mother's passing Elias decides to close the shop, he has no drive or motivation to work. In the past week he hasn't gotten out of bed before ten in the morning and hangs around the house doing very little apart from watching television, smoking his pipe, and drinking arak. This is unusual because he has always been an early riser and a very hard worker, he rarely ever smoked and only drank alcohol at dinner time. He feels very down most of the time and doesn't really understand why, he thought for sure he would feel nothing but peace after Nadeem's passing. All his stepfather ever did was make him feel useless, so he struggles to understand why he feels sadness rather than solace. Elias is depressed but has no insight into his condition, he has never talked about his feelings and was not about to start, so this elephant in the room remains, but it is unsettling for him.

A month passes and things have not improved, in fact Elias has not returned to the shop. Mary is worried about him; he has never kept the shop closed for this long. She knows he is not doing very well; she has more insight into conditions like this since her son's diagnosis. She tries to encourage her husband to go outside and sit near the garden and enjoy the fresh air hoping this might help, but he refuses to leave the house. She is now at her wits end because there is nothing, she can do to help lift his mood, he just mopes around the house doing nothing all day. Watching over her husband has impacted on her daily visits to Claudia and Eli, she only sees them twice a week now and is extremely unhappy about that, something must be done.

One day Mary has an idea, and she leaves the house early in the morning returning only a few hours later. Upon her return she finds Elias sitting in front of the television watching old westerns like he has been doing for months. He glances over at Mary as she enters through the front door and is shocked, surprised and elated all at once to discover she is carrying Eli in her arms. Smiling with pure joy he leaps to his feet and races over to see his precious baby grandson for the first time. He takes Eli from Mary's arms instantly showering him with kisses, his eyes filled with tears of happiness. Eli suddenly belts out a loud cry, spooked and terrified by this stranger. This does not deter his grandfather who continues to shower the poor baby with kisses, but Mary stands by closely, so Eli doesn't threat too much. After a while the baby settles and begins to watch this strange man in wonder. The baby, just through his sheer presence, has helped lift a dark cloud that has hung over his grandfather for months.

Hours pass and Mary must take Eli back to his mother, but Elias looks so happy, something she hasn't seen in a very long time. She knows how much he'll want to see his grandson again, but he won't say that he's too proud, but she has a plan.

'I will ask Claudia if I can bring him back tomorrow if you want?' She speaks in Arabic which is how they both still communicate at home.

'If you want to bring him, you can.' He insists like a stubborn mule.

So, she talks Claudia into allowing another visit knowing how much this will mean to her depressed and stubborn husband. Surprisingly Claudia does not object, in fact she is delighted that her father wants to see his grandson. She is also thrilled because it gives her much needed free time to do all the things, she can't do with a baby around. She hopes her father will eventually come to visit but like Mary, Claudia is not pushing it.

He now has something to live for again, he has so much love to give to this tiny baby. Elias is overcome by Mary's kindness; she didn't need to do this for him. He has been terrible to her for so many years, yet she lifted him from a place of deep sadness, and he wishes he could undo all the wrongs of the past that had made her life miserable. There are still intermittent periods of sadness that come and go when he thinks about the past, it's hard to forget the harshness of his upbringing at the hands of his merciless stepfather. He also dwells on the foolish mistakes he has made by spending way too much time in the shop rather than with his family, all for the sake of making much more money than needed. He missed being a part of his family's life to make Nadeem proud, but he tries hard not to think about it and buries those thoughts deep, praying for another chance now that he has Eli in his life.

For the first time in months things start to look brighter for Elias and he decides to take another month off from working at the shop. He has never taken this much time off before and wonders if perhaps it's now time to live his life a little differently. He asks his nephew Paul to run the shop, sadly his nephew is just like his father Anton, always in and out of work, and so out of pity he gives him the job. He thinks this is the least he can do for his poor sister Zahra who has had to put up with Anton, a terrible husband. Although Paul is not a great store manager, at least the shop is open again. Elias starts to garden for the first time since he left Lebanon all those years ago. He wants to straighten up the backyard so it will be safe for Eli to run around when he starts to walk.

The month pass very quickly, and Elias is not ready to go back to work, so he decides to take more time off. If things were different between father and son, he would call it quits and hand the business over to Joseph, but the relationship is so fractured that it is not an option. He hopes that maybe someday there can be peace between them but knows that's not likely, he must lay in the bed he made. Accordingly, he has no choice but to keep his nephew on even though he is lazy and not great for business, he wants to spend more time with Eli and is happy to pay the price for it.

Another positive turn of events for Elias is the improvement in his and Mary's relationship. They spend a lot of time together these days, sometimes sitting for hours on the veranda under the morning sun talking about the old country, family and politics, a typical pass time for the Lebanese. It's been years since he has thought about his old life in Lebanon, the past forty years have come and gone so quickly. All those long hours in the shop trying to build a better life for his family may have been in vain, it tied-up a chunk of his adult life and he missed out on so many precious memories of his children growing up.

Charbel and Nayla often come by to visit Elias at his house, unfortunately Hilda refuses to go because she has never been able to forgive her brother-in-law for what he did to her husband. Even so, the visits are bittersweet, of course he loves seeing his siblings, but their presence is a constant reminder of his cowardice actions that separated a mother from her beloved children. However, he is the only one that feels this way, Charbel and Nayla don't see it like that, they love their brother and always look forward to seeing him. Zahra and Samya come to see him occasionally, but their husbands discourage their visits, unwilling to associate with a family that broke ties with tradition, Leila, and Claudia in particular. Even with Nadeem and the other traditional patriarchs long gone to their graves, the cruel social mores persist.

Elias now takes Mary to visit her ageing parents each week and they are overjoyed to see their daughter smiling again, they have noted subtle changes in their son-in-law as well. Mary relishes in these visits as her parents are very old and frail now, so she wants to spend as much time as she can with them. In the past they avoided coming to her house unwilling to see Elias, deeply resentful of the way he treated their daughter. Mary in turn couldn't visit them because she was too busy raising her children unassisted. In the past this arrangement suited Elias well because rather than entertain guests all he wanted to do was eat and relax after a long day at work. So, he never cared to socialise apart from the obligatory visits to Nadeem and Leila's house each Sunday when they were alive. Mary is puzzled by the changes in her husband, but she embraces it none the less, their marriage is happy for a change and that's enough for her.

Lately Claudia has been dropping Eli off at her parents' house so they can spend time with their grandson, she stays to chat a little and is surprised that her father engages in the conversations she has with her mother. As time goes on her visits extend from minutes into hours and Claudia starts to see how much her father has softened, she hopes that one day he might accept his children for the way they live their life. The truth is Elias doesn't understand them or agree with how they live their life, but he does begin to accept that it is their way of life. There are no apologies from either of them, father and daughter simply begin to speak again, and Claudia is ok with that.

Elias understands that mending relationships with the rest of his children will take a lot of time, perhaps it will never happen. He doesn't ask Claudia about her siblings but does give her a large wad of cash to give to Leila for her recent marriage to Scott. He also gives Claudia money for herself and extra cash to give to Nada and Joseph. This is by far the biggest change Mary has seen in her husband, money used to be as important to him as the air is to breath.

For the first time in a long while husband and wife begin to feel genuine affection for one another again. Elias has always loved his wife, although has never made much effort to show it. He adored Mary back in the day when they first married, but the sentiment vanished as he began to focus way too much on work hoping to impress Nadeem. Neglecting his own family to please his stepfather drove a wedge between the couple and their marriage deteriorated over time. With

Nadeem gone the married couple seem to have rekindled a spark in their relationship, something not felt for a very long time.

Just when things look brighter between husband and wife, that soon changes for the worse. Even so, at least for now their marriage is almost as happy as it was in the very early days. Tonight, Mary has prepared her husband one of his favourite dishes, kibbeh nayeh, he devours his meal in no time, but notices Mary hasn't eaten anything on her plate.

'Why don't you eat?' He asks.

'I'm not hungry, I still have the headache from this morning.' She sighs, the pain is bad.

'Take Panadol, you'll feel better.' He insists.

'I already have, maybe I'll rest on the coach, let me clear the table for you.'

'No, you rest, I can take care of it.' He seems a little concerned.

Mary smiles gratefully at the man she lost years ago, but she is glad to have him back.

Elias cleans up and then joins Mary on the couch. She has fallen asleep, so he doesn't disturb her and watches the news instead.

An hour passes and he notices Mary hasn't stirred so he decides to wake her so she can go upstairs and sleep more solidly in bed.

'Mary, Mary wake up.' He pokes her shoulder to awaken her, but she doesn't stir. He pokes her shoulder a few times, but she doesn't respond.

'Mary, Mary, wake up.' He raises his voice beginning to panic.

Elias shakes Mary's arm hoping that will stir her, but there is no response. He races to the phone and calls an ambulance and then calls Claudia. By now her body has stumped over on the couch but Elias still tries to stir her from this worrying sleep. He keeps shaking her hoping she'll miraculously wake up, but she doesn't, and his entire body trembles in fear. Shocked to the core he can't believe this is happening, hoping he has fallen asleep unknowingly and that this is just a terrible dream. Claudia arrives before the ambulance and has brought Leila along with her. Leila races over to her mother wanting to check on her but can't because Elias won't let go of Mary.

'Please, let me check on her.' Leila begs him in Arabic.

Overcome with shock he nods in a daze hoping Leila can miraculously heal Mary. She talks to her mother trying to get a response, but there is none. She checks Mary's pulse and breathing but the vital signs are not there, there is no sign of life. Leila loses her composure, and suddenly bursts into tears because she knows they have lost her, she's gone. And with that, she goes from a restrained and measured medical doctor to a heartbroken, grief stricken and terrified daughter. The ambulance arrives to take over but it's too late. Mary never regains consciousness; she tragically passes away from a brain aneurysm.

When Mary passes Elias goes back to the shop, the devastating loss is hard to cope with and work distract him, the darkness hanging over him comes and goes when he doesn't have time to think about it. Six months after her passing he continues to spend every waking hour in the shop and only goes home to eat and sleep. That being the case his garden grows wild and remains unkept, the lawn is ten inches high and full of weeds. Inside his house it's just as bad, the kitchen sink is overfilled with dirty dishes, other dirty plates and cups are left lying all over the kitchen and lounge room. His clothes smell and the bed sheets haven't been changed in months. All that Mary did around the house has been taken for granted which makes him feel very guilty.

He doesn't want to be at home anymore because it reminds him too much of his wife, a big change of heart from someone that treated her so poorly for decades. After just a few years together Elias and Mary's marriage soured but they stayed together for their children and more to the point to honour their custom which forbade divorce. The very notion of a marriage break up was simply out of the question, and so they merely coexisted for a very long time. Despite this, they remained companions, although not great ones, and relied on one another for company, especially when the children left home. And although their relationship had soured, it improved a lot towards the end of Mary's life. Now he is forced to live in a house full of memories, good and bad and struggles to overcome feelings of extreme loneliness.

The mess and stench of dirty dishes and clothing, as well his unkept garden begins to bother him. After much deliberation Elias decides to get a small granny flat built at the back of his shop so he can move into it and leave this large and lonely home behind, the flat would be much easier to manage plus he would be able cook and clean during the quieter times of trade. Importantly, it means he can avoid living in a house that is a constant reminder of Mary whom he misses terribly. The house also holds awful memories of how poorly he treated his wife and children over many years, that is something he wants to try hard to forget.

Months later Elias receives a surprising and much welcome visit from Claudia when she stops by at the shop with Eli. When he sees his grandson his heart leaps with joy and no amount of pride can disguise it. It's late afternoon and he closes the shop two hours early because he is so excited to see Eli. He has also missed Claudia but won't freely admit it, even so it is written all over his face. She has also missed her father and is very happy to see him. Although still suffering terrible grief since her mother's passing, she realises her father is getting old and wants to be there for him, that's certainly something her mother would have wanted.

He cuddles and kisses Eli who cries out to his mother, too much time has passed for him to remember his grandfather, a painful reminder of lost time. Elias smiles at his grandson as he reaches into his pocket to hand him a chocolate bar. Eli looks puzzled by the package; he has no idea what it is.

'Dad don't give him chocolate, his only just turned one.' She insists speaking English.

'I'll get him a meat pie; poor boy must be hungry.' Elias responds in English.

Claudia doesn't have the heart to tell him no, so she nods politely.

'I'll make you a sandwich, I have fresh bread and salami delivered today.' He insists.

'I'm fine because I already ate.' She insists politely, feeling terrible knowing it is rude to turn food down in their culture.

'Please eat something.' He insists.

'I'll eat the chocolate bar.' She smiles.

Elias quickly disappears to gather the pie and returns, handing it to Claudia so she can feed Eli.

'He can have it in a little while, let it cool off.' She has no intention of feeding her son the meat pie.

'Ok, then I want to show you something.' He says with a hint of excitement. 'Come with me.'

He leads the way and Claudia follows with Eli in her arms. They enter a newly built flat which is now attached to the shop, Claudia looks surprised not expecting to see this.

'Come and sit at the table so you can give Eli some pie to eat.' He leads her over to a small dinner table. Once they are seated Elias begins to play with Eli. Claudia smiles, it's hard to stay angry at her father.

'Why did you decide to have this built? What's wrong with your house?' She asks.

He doesn't answer and continues to play with his grandson instead. Claudia knows her father is a stubborn man who struggles to show any emotions and feelings, but she pushes him on the subject.

'It's ok to miss mum, there's nothing wrong with that.' She insists.

He looks uncomfortable because he doesn't want to talk about it.

'We all miss her dad; we loved her very much.'

Elias looks at Claudia solemnly but doesn't say anything. Claudia shakes her head ready to give up on him.

'I wasn't the best to her I know, your mother was a very good woman, she loved you all very much.'

'I know.' She tries hard not to cry; the loss is painful and hard to come to terms with.

'I have been a terrible husband and father, and the house has too many bad memories. So, I live here now.'

They both sit in silence filled with deep sadness.

I can't change the past, I must live with it, at least in this flat it's a bit easier. Anyway, I want to talk to you about something else, about the house.'

'What about it?' She looks puzzled.

'I want to give it to all my children. You can all move into it now and don't waste money on rent anymore.' Claudia can't believe what's she's hearing, so surprised by the offer she doesn't know what to say.

'What? Really?' She's overwhelmed.

'I want you all to have a place to live and now Eli will grow up with all the things he needs. I don't want any of you to struggle.'

He never wants his children to experience poverty the way he did, this would safeguard his children and his grandson from ever encountering anything like the life he had in Lebanon.

'That's very generous dad.' Overcome with joy she smiles as her eyes fill with tears of happiness. The past year has been challenging with all the cost of rent and food, even though Nada has covered most of it, it's been a struggle.' She can't believe it and is overcome with emotion. Elias smiles, this brings him as much joy as it does for her.

'What else do you want to eat, come on.' He insists.

'I'll have one of your salami and tomato rolls, the roll with sesame seeds and butter on it as well.' She smiles at him.

He happily gets up to prepare the food and disappears back into the shop. Claudia can't stop smiling, feeling a great sense of relief that she and Eli finally have a place to call home, not just some where to stay until she gets back onto to her feet. For the first time she feels proud of her father, and to show her appreciation she makes a pledge to herself that she will look after him as he ages. Deep down she knows she'll have to because the other kids won't, there's just too much hurt that they can't put behind them.

Mary's passing is devastating for the whole family, not least of all her children. They struggle terribly to come to terms with the loss of their mother. Mary's sudden and unexpected death shatters an impermeable tie they had with their mother. She formed a steely bond with her children, and that tie grew stronger over the years, nurtured by her devotion and unconditional love for her precious children. She was always there for them growing up, while Elias was invariably in the shop. She fed them, nursed them through sickness, played with them, cried with them, and she did it selflessly and without any help. Her children were her life, her light and she loved them dearly. And so, with their mother gone they come to realise how much she gave up and the guilt hits hard. They deeply regret not spending more time with her and helping around the house. They saw how tough their mother had it but never took time to show gratitude for the endless acts of selflessness and unbounded love. Even so, it's too late now and so they feel overwhelmed by guilt and despair.

The children know Elias has become depressed since Mary's passing, but apart from Claudia they show little to no pity. They struggle to forgive him for the way he treated their mother throughout their marriage, and for the way he treated them. Mary brought her kids up close and in grief they bond together even tighter, forcing Elias further out of their circle, and sadly at a time that he needs them the most. Claudia is the only child who has any empathy for him, the visits she made to her mother and father with Eli opened her eyes up to see a softer and kinder side to him.

When Nadeem died and Elias spiralled into a deep depression, it was Mary who helped lift him out of it, despite his reluctance to acknowledge his condition and do something about it. She persevered and found a way to help him, because she cared deeply for her husband, despite years of unhappiness between them. Now there is nobody, perhaps Claudia but she is dealing with her own grief and has kept busy with her young child.

Elias can't move beyond his loss, even with the luxury of a new and conveniently located flat away from his old house filled with painful memories and despite the treasured visits he enjoys from Claudia and Eli, he feels empty and sad without his wife. Although their marriage was not great for many years, they were still companions for more than forty years and he has lost that. All he has now is an empty flat filled with loneliness and grief. Too proud to call Claudia and ask to see

Eli more often, he just keeps working hoping the pain will eventually fade away.

The months that follow are a blur as he continues to work in the shop, the daily grind and long hours beat up his ageing body, he simply doesn't have the strength and stamina of the years gone by. The occasional visit from his brother brightens up his day but soon these drop off due to Charbel's failing health, making it hard for him to come see Elias. Nayla tries to visit occasionally but she is also getting old and frail, most of her time is dedicated to the Church. His other sisters pop in once or twice every couple of months but they are busy with their grandchildren. Apart from Claudia, none of his children visit him.

Although Claudia struggles with the loss of her beloved mother, there is light in her life, and that is Eli. Without the love and joy that he brings into her day, the grief would be a lot worse. The renewed father daughter relationship is also nice, and she still can't believe the generosity her father has shown by offering her a house to live in. She is very eager to move, looking forward to having a room for just her and Eli, rather than share with her younger sister. Nada is also keen to move back into the old family home, relieved that half her pay won't be swallowed up in rent anymore. Claudia wants the whole family to move back, but Leila and Scott decline the offer preferring to have a house of their own now that they are expecting their first child. Joseph decides it's time to leave Leila and Scott, especially with the impending birth of their child, and so he also decides to move back along with Claudia, Nada, and Eli.

After giving the house a thorough clean, applying fresh paint, pulling up the old carpet and giving the backyard a much-needed pruning, the siblings and Eli move back into the family home. Joseph's mental health has continued to improve, and he has kept the same job for a few years now. He still struggles with his social phobia but has just learnt to live with it. Sadly, he refuses to have anything to do with his father. Nada is in a relationship but is not ready to settle down, so she is happy to stay with her siblings for now. She has started to visit her father occasionally, tagging along with Claudia. Sometimes Leila joins them, but Joseph refuses to see his father. True to her word Claudia visits her father daily, of course with Eli in tow.

As the years roll on Elias continues to struggle with managing the shop, to cope he drops his trading hours and no longer opens on the weekend. He doesn't have the appetite for business anymore and lacks the drive that used to possess him, the older he gets the less important money is to him. He wishes he had Mary with him now so they could enjoy this new life together, but she isn't coming back. Apart from the visits from Claudia and Eli and occasionally from Nada and Leila, he has nothing apart from the shop, and so he keeps working.

It has been months since Charbel has come to visit, so Elias decides to go and see him one weekend. When he arrives at Charbel's house Hilda greets him with a frosty smile, she can't warm up to him. On entering their home, he looks shocked to see Charbel in a wheelchair, he knew his brother was unwell but not to this extent. Hilda leaves the room to allow them time to catch up because it's been a while since the brothers have seen one another.

'What happened to you?' He asks Charbel.

'I'm ok, don't worry, it is part of the illness, but everything is ok. Tell me how the children are?' He asks, trying to change the subject to avoid talking about his deteriorating health.

'Brother, why don't you tell me the truth? Elias won't back down.

'It's from the asbestos, it was right throughout the factory. Who would have known sweeping the factory floor could be so harmful.' He sighs.

Elias looks devastated hearing this and doesn't know what to say. He clears his throat trying to contain his emotions, not wanting to upset his brother.

'It should be me; you have been nothing but a saint, a good husband, father and a very good brother, I'm the one that should be sick, Father in Heaven why not me?' Elias stares sadly at the ceiling half expecting a sign from God. Extremely distressed by the tragic news, he must sit down. Accordingly, he slowly eases himself into a chair next to his brother to take the weight off his weak and unsteady legs.

'Stop talking like that. Your life from the beginning has been cursed, born into poverty, losing your father so young, and having him replaced by a tyrant like my father, I would have been just like you.' Charbel insists empathetically.

'See how kind you are, why did this happen to you?' Elias wipes his teary eyes.

'It's ok, this life is not forever, we all come and go.' Charbel tries to comfort his brother.

'That's what our mother always said.'

'And it's true.' Charbel smiles.

'But even though all of us will be called away in time, it's the ones that are left behind who ache with grief because they miss their loved ones.' Elias stares sadly at his brother and Charbel nods understanding completely.

'Where are your children?' The conversation is too painful, so Elias changes the subject.

'Long gone.' Charbel laughs. 'They're fully grown with families of their own.'

'They should be with you, helping.' He insists.

'They come when they can. It's hard because they work and must look after their own children.' He explains.

'I don't understand the Australian way.' Elias insists.

'I'm ok.' Charbel smiles at his brother as he tries to reassure him.' What about you, how are your children?'

'Joseph still doesn't talk to me.' He admits despairingly. 'But Claudia visits all the time, she's kind like her mother. The others are not so forgiving.' He stares sadly at his brother.

'Give them time, it's a different generation and they are nothing like us. They never grew up in the way we did, that's something you never accepted.' Charbel insists treading carefully, hoping not to judge his brother too harshly.

'Life in Lebanon was much simpler, and children respected their parents.' He insists.

'Look at what the old ways of Lebanon did to me and your sister. This is not Lebanon, and in many ways I'm glad, because the culture was not always kind either.' He insists and Elias nods solemnly.

Elias smiles at his brother wanting to say something but his pride holds him back. Charbel stares at him patiently allowing him time to open up.

'You always knew what was most important.' Elias confides choked up. 'You were the younger brother, but you knew, but I couldn't see it. On the ship all those years ago, you could see money was not so important, and that love was. The young one and the smart one.' Elias smiles at his brother as he wipes a tear from his eyes.

'You were smarter than me.' Charbel smiles at him. 'You just made a mistake, we all do it.'

'I will come and visit you more often, I've missed you brother.' Elias smiles at Charbel lovingly. The brothers continue to talk until it is late. Elias promises to visit, and he honours that, but sadly those gatherings end far too soon.

Charbel passes away just a few months later and it's another blow for Elias. His brother was his closest companion for many years, before either of them married. He reminisces back to their days of adventure crossing the sea, on route to the new world, setting up a home for the family to come and join them. They were tough years but good years. Elias begins to feel like there isn't much left to live for, but he still looks forward to seeing Eli, this keeps him going.

A few years later Elias finally closes the shop for trade, by now he can no longer manage on his own, and there is no one to take over the business. He is seventy-four years of age, an amazing feat to have worked this long, and if his health wasn't failing him, he would probably push on a little longer. With nothing else to do, other than hold out for his daily visits from Claudia and Eli, what else is there to do, so work has been a good distraction to boredom and loneliness, but now his health is too poor.

He has suffered dizzy spells on and off over the past six months and Leila wants him to get a blood test. Predictably stubborn he refuses, but in the end relents when Leila threatens to stop visiting him. In the past Elias would have shrugged off the threat, but he has changed a lot and doesn't want to risk losing her again. Leila suspects her father is diabetic and the testing confirms her this, it's a big blow for Elias, he has never had to watch his diet or take medication. The few pleasures in life of late, food and his arak are taken away. This will be one more thing for Claudia to monitor, her sisters are too busy with work to help, and Leila now has two children of her own to care for on top of her other commitments.

Elias decides he does not want to sell his business, he'd rather keep the shop unoccupied because he doesn't want a new business owner working so closely to his home. Deep down though, it has more to do with his inability to let go of a business, it has formed a major part of his life, he can't accept a new owner replacing what he had built from nothing and has run for over forty years.

As the years go by his shop remains closed and unkept, and it starts to look more and more derelict with each day. The original bushel's tea sign above the shop entrance has faded with the old paint flaking away, shelving in the store has gathered thick dust, the old fridges still stand but are empty and covered in webs, his shop has become a picture of the past.

Claudia continues to visit her father daily, usually around 9 am to help him shower and get dressed, she also cooks his meals and checks his blood sugar levels. Lately Elias has refused to take his medication because he has lost his will to live, he has become so frail and sick that he doesn't enjoy life anymore, and the older he gets the more he misses the family that has passed before him. His memory is failing too, so Claudia begs him to move back in with the family so she can watch over him closely, but he refuses to do that to Joseph, still regretting daily how badly he treated his son. Eli is 10 years old now and he often does his homework at his grandfather's flat while Claudia cooks and cleans for her father. Leila tries to bring her children over occasionally which brightens up her father's day, sadly he is too frail to hold them, which is heartbreaking for both.

Each morning he still wakes early, just like he had done for decades, when the shop was trading. Even though his store has been closed for a very long time, he still manages to make his way into the shop in the early hours of the morning, made possible with the aid of his walking frame. He sits in the dark by a dimly lit lamp, still dressed in his night clothes, Claudia has no idea about this morning ritual.

He sits and stares at the wall thinking about the past, reminiscing about his life in Lebanon, both good and bad times. He recalls sad moments as a very young child when Nadeem would lash out at him for no good reason, but he also remembers nice times when he and Charbel would race down lush green mountainous slopes, his brother could never keep up with him. He remembers his mother fondly and then his poor dear wife that suffered so much because of him. He dwells on the past and those memories play out like a movie, recalling each scene of his life leading up to this point.

On this morning he feels especially unwell, lightheaded, and dizzy. Even so, he doesn't care, he has had enough of this life. He wants to go and be with his mother and his brother and of course Mary, life has become very lonely indeed. As he gets dizzier the lights begin to dim and suddenly everything goes black.

Elias lays in a hospital bed, falling in and out of consciousness. Claudia and Eli sit by his bedside terrified that he may never recover from the massive stroke he has suffered. Claudia found her father lying unconscious on the shop floor this morning and blames herself for not being there sooner. She wished he had not been so stubborn and agreed to move in with them, so he could be cared for in the way he needed. The thought of it eats away at her as she sits anxiously by his bedside not sure if he will make it. She blames herself, why didn't she do more for him? If she forced him to take his medication this probably would never have happened. Claudia has grown very close to her father, they always had a special connection, she was hoping to spend many more years with him, and now she may not.

Leila enters the room shocked to see her father in such a serious state of poor health. She struggles to imagine him weak like this, when he was always so strong and healthy, and now he can barely breath. The sisters embrace tightly, and Leila kisses her nephew. She goes over to see her father and watches him momentarily before bursting into tears.

'I can't believe it, such a stubborn man.' She sighs wiping her tears.

'He stopped taking his medication, I tried so hard to get him to take it and he wouldn't.' Claudia insists as she sobs.

'You did so much for him, there was nothing more you could do to make him take it. Such a stubborn man.' Leila insists. She stares sadly at her father, despite all the bad times, he was still her father and she loved him.

'I'm glad he had you with him after mum died, at least he wasn't completely alone.' Leila remarks.

Nada enters the room with Nayla trailing slowly behind her niece. Even at this age and as a retired nun, she continues to dress in her habit. Extremely frail, she slowly paces towards her brother's bedside kissing his forehead and placing rosary beads onto his chest. She begins to chant the Our Father as Elias lays lifelessly in his bed, there is no way of telling whether he can hear or see her. Nada hugs and kisses her father as she sobs along with her sisters.

'Will Joseph come?' Claudia asks Nada.

'I begged him, told him dad doesn't have much longer, but he won't see him.' She insists solemnly.

They all watch him sadly, aware that he is slipping away.

Later that night Elias lays deathly still in his hospital bed, his breathing is very shallow. Claudia is asleep on the couch, refusing to leave him alone, and the rest of the family left a few hours ago. As Claudia sleeps, Elias takes his last breath.

Suddenly the door opens, and Leila enters the room, she walks over to her son and kisses him on his cheek, he opens his eyes smiling joyfully.

'Mother, how can you be alive?' He asks in confusion.

'It's time son.' She smiles at him.

'I don't understand.' He insists.

'Close your eyes and take my hand, trust me, and trust in God.'

Elias closes his eyes, and suddenly he feels a warmth like the autumn sun passing right through his body. The room is as bright as the sun, and he feels a quiet calmness like never before. He doesn't know if he is alive or dead, but when he finds himself standing next to his mother, brother, and wife in the beautiful mountains of Lebanon he realises, he is finally at peace.

The next day they gather at the old family home to prepare for their father's funeral, anticipating a flood of guests that will soon fill their home for the wake. Extended family and members of the old community will come to offer condolences and prayer to Elias and the family he has left behind.

Joseph refuses to come downstairs to join them and stays in his room. He lays in bed confused and upset by the events of the day, feeling guilty for not going to see his father. He couldn't bring himself to go, the hurt and anger was too deep-rooted. He closes his eyes hoping to fall asleep, not wanting to feel the anguish anymore, it takes a while, but he slips into a shallow sleep, so when he suddenly hears his father's voice Joseph doesn't know if he is dreaming or not. Startled, Joseph awakens confused by what he may have just heard. Looking around the room he doesn't see anything, so he closes his eyes hoping this is a bad dream.

'Son.' Elias calls out softly to Joseph.

Joseph can now see his father and he trembles in fear. Elias looks young again, and very happy.

'Don't be scared.' He tells his son.

Joseph is terrified and thinks he has gone mad.

'I'm here to tell you something, please try not to be afraid. Trust me son.' Elias stares lovingly at Joseph who begins to relax.

'I am sorry for how I treated you, I was a terrible father, but I always loved you. I hope you can forgive me because I want you to find peace.' He speaks softly and calmly, with genuine love. Suddenly there is a knock on the door which snaps Joseph out of his sleep.

'Let me in Joseph.' Claudia calls out from behind the closed door.

He quickly looks around the room but can no longer see his father, Elias is gone. Claudia barges into the room, worried for her brother and goes to him, suddenly Joseph hugs her tightly, and the rare sign of affection surprises her. He holds her tightly unwilling to let go.

'Are you ok?' Claudia asks.

'Yeah, I think so.' He smiles nervously, but at the same time he feels a sense of peace, unlike ever before.

* * *